One Shenandoah Winter

A Novel

T. Davis Bunn

THOMAS NELSON PUBLISHERS
Nashville

Published in Nashville, Tennessee, by Thomas Nelson, Inc., Publishers.

Library of Congress Cataloging-in-Publication Data

Bunn, T. Davis, 1952–

One Shenandoah Winter: a novel / T. Davis Bunn.

p. cm.

ISBN 0-7852-7217-8

I. Title.

PS3552.U4718056 1998

813'.54—dc21

98-19987

CIP

Printed in the United States of America.

1 2 3 4 5 6 BVG 03 02 01 00 99 98

This book is dedicated to

JANETTE OKE

Whose friendship remains a brilliant beacon.

So teach us to number our days,
that we may apply our hearts unto wisdom.
Psalm 90:12 KJV

Autumn 1961

One

The first thing Connie saw when she rounded the final rise was Dawn waiting out in front of the house, her golden hair shining in the sun like a crown. The sight was enough to hollow out Connie's chest. How beautiful the girl was, and how full of life. But that was not what saddened Connie. The evening before, the first time they had seen one another in two long months, they had quarreled. And of all the topics Connie could have argued over, she had chosen to criticize Dawn's boyfriend. As though Connie's lonely life granted her any right whatsoever to give advice about men.

Dawn waved like she had since she was six, when Connie

had started picking her up on the way into town. As usual, Dawn's parents had left two hours earlier. Hattie and Chad Campbell ran Hillsboro's only grocery, and a life of longer hours Connie had yet to find. Dawn waved with her hand high over her head and used her entire body to put emphasis behind the greeting. The straight yellow hair swayed back and forth, and rippled like water pouring down a golden waterfall.

Connie Wilkes slowed to grant herself time to swallow the gouging sadness. Such silliness was not permitted on a beautiful early-October morning. Especially when there was absolutely nothing to be done about anything. Dawn had been spending time with Duke Langdon for almost a year now, and it was her choice. Life was just that way.

The brakes on her uncle's old pickup shuddered as Connie stopped. Most young people would have called the heap an absolute embarrassment and refused to be seen dead inside. But Dawn opened her door and smiled her way into the seat, then took a deep breath and declared, "Still smells like Poppa Joe. Wet dogs and strong tobacco and gun oil."

"I think that's why I keep it," Connie agreed. Poppa Joe was her uncle, a cantakerous mountain man who had bought the truck in Connie's fourteenth year. "It reminds me of how happy I was 'way back when.'"

"Me too." Dawn Campbell bounced up and down on the seat, making the old springs squeak a tired welcome. She used both hands to crank down the window, the motions coming easy with years of practice. "I like to remember times with Poppa Joe when things get me down."

"Honey, you're too young to have a past and too pretty for bad memories." Connie searched the empty road ahead and behind, then was caught by the look Dawn gave her. It was far too ancient to be coming from such a vibrant face. "What?"

"Nothing, Aunt Connie. The road's clear." But the look held on, telling Connie that the young girl beside her was growing up a lot faster than Connie might have liked.

Connie grasped the gearshift lever and yanked it up into first. The truck was twenty-five years old and had done a hundred-fifty-five thousand miles, most of them over hills and gravel tracks. The engine had been rebored six times, the shocks and brakes replaced more often than Connie cared to think. The radio and the passenger windshield wiper didn't work, the lights jounced and jiggled with every bump, and the paint had long been scraped off by passing branches and shrubs. The hood was rounded and a mile long, and she needed a thick cushion to protect her back from the springs sticking through the old seat covers. But the truck was a part of almost every good memory she held, and many of those not so good. As long as she could, Connie was going to keep the old heap on the road.

Dawn was twenty and the daughter of Connie's oldest friend. She had grown from an angel of a little girl into the darling of Hillsboro, Virginia, and everyone who knew her wished there were some way to keep her from spreading her wings and flying away, Connie most of all.

Dawn gave her a smile that twisted her heart and said, "Today's the big day!"

Connie nodded, knowing she should be happy finally to have landed a doctor for her town, yet surprised to find her earlier sadness still present. The unwanted emotion remained stationed right there between them. But the idea of an older man like Duke Langdon making time with her darling Dawn rankled so much it felt as if she had eaten a jar of pickles with her breakfast coffee.

True, Duke was only twenty-nine, but he had an air about him that made him seem much older. He was far too handsome for his own good. He was also as rich as anyone could be in a small Shenandoah Valley town. Connie had long suspected that behind those sparkling eyes and cleft chin resided a very large vacuum. She could just see him now, smug in his knowledge that he could have any girl he wanted, only to brush her aside whenever the magic faded.

Her worry and her anger fueled the look she gave Dawn then. A look meant to find something to criticize. And Connie did not have to look very far. The year of 1961 was more than halfway over, and already this strange new decade threatened to change everything and everybody, whether they wanted change or not. The lowland papers were full of what they called the rock-and-roll era. Pictures showed boys in ducktails and stovepipe jeans jiving with girls in bobby socks, ponytails, and petticoats. And lipstick as red as Dawn's. "Does your mother mind you laying the makeup on like a woman twice your age?"

Dawn gave her hair an irritated tug. "Don't you start."

"I take it that means yes."

"I'll tell you the same thing I told her. Get used to it. My makeup is just fine, thank you."

There was something new in her voice. After a moment of dragging the truck around a hairpin curve, Connie realized what it was. Dawn sounded exactly like Connie did when she was angry. The person beside her was no longer a child, but an irritated woman. Grown and aware and certain of herself. Connie said quietly, "Yes, you're right. It's just fine."

"Be glad it's not jewelry I can only wear when I've got holes in my ears," Dawn huffed.

"You can stop arguing with your mother now," Connie said.

"You started it."

"And I'm sorry." But the tension remained in the air between them. "I was still mad when you got in. I apologize."

The words surprised them both. It was the first time she had ever spoken to Dawn as an adult. The knowledge occupied Connie's mind and heart as they descended the hillside toward town. Not even last night, when they had quarreled over her keeping company with Duke Langdon, had Connie seen this person beside her as a woman. It jolted her to think this was what the row might really have been about.

Dawn had been attending Mountainview Junior College for two years now. The Jonestown campus was twenty-five miles away as the crow flew, but only if the crow could crest the highland ridges that separated the two valleys. For the earthbound traveler it was a ninety-minute drive along winding Appalachian roads. This summer Dawn had gone straight from Jonestown to Richmond, where she had attended four months of classes at the business college. After acing every course, she had returned home the previous weekend and announced she was going to stop with college entirely. Attending the more distant university was out.

Which was what had started the argument. Connie was certain Dawn had decided against attending university because she wanted to be close to Duke Langdon. Connie's loudly stated opinion that no man was worth such a sacrifice, most especially Duke, had not exactly gone over well.

Dawn gave her a sideways look, not certain that things really had progressed beyond her makeup. "Does this mean we're through with what we started on last night, Aunt Connie?"

"I won't talk about it any more," Connie agreed, though admitting defeat was hard. She had never been good at losing anything, especially an argument.

Dawn nodded, turned back to the road, and said to the windshield, "I prayed last night and again this morning that things would be right between us. I don't like it when we quarrel. It makes my whole world feel out of joint."

"Mine too." But Connie was held by the news of having been prayed over. The words had come so easily to Dawn. Connie tried to think of the last time she had actually turned a problem over to God, but she could not remember. It left her unable to run from an honest reply. "I think I've been partly arguing with myself and not with you. For everything that isn't right in my life."

"Like what, Aunt Connie?"

She gave Hattie Campbell's daughter as much of a smile as she could manage. "I think it's time you started calling me Connie. To have an *adult* call me aunt makes me feel ancient."

Dawn accepted the statement with a thoughtful nod, but only said, "What's the matter with your life?" When Connie did not respond, she went on, "I've always thought I'd like to turn out just like you."

Connie shot a glance at herself in the rearview mirror, for her reply was to be shared only with herself. On a good day she would have called herself attractive, but today was not that kind. She accepted the copper-blonde hair and the clear green eyes and the strong chin and the warm-toned complexion with a sort of commonplace satisfaction. What caused her to turn back to the road was the sadness she saw layered over it all.

The road lifted up and over the last hill, and the valley of Hillsboro opened up before them. The narrow lowlands contained a cluster of buildings, most of them dating back to the early decades of the century. Back in the teens and twenties, their local stone was considered as fine a construction material as marble. Many of the Richmond government buildings were finished with polished slabs of Hillsboro granite. The resulting flush of money had spurred a building spree, when every structure from the local courthouse to Langdon's Emporium had competed for small-town grandeur.

Then the Great Depression had struck, and the demand for Hillsboro granite dried up. Afterward, when the rest of the world began to accelerate once again, Hillsboro had remained locked in the same destitute gap that trapped it today. Going nowhere fast.

But today was one of those special moments in the Appalachians, when hardship had no place. The air was scrubbed a fine china blue, and the hillsides were a thousand hues of green. Down the center of the valley flowed a sparkling silver ribbon, known to all as the Shenandoah River.

"Did you hear what I said?"

"I heard." Connie's slow reply hung heavy with all that she could not put into words. Not ever. Especially not to Dawn. "Thank you very much for the compliment, but I wouldn't wish my own state on anyone, much less you."

"But why?" Dawn's consternation was genuine. "You're, gosh, you're great. Successful, independent, respected by almost everybody in town."

For years now, Connie had been paid by the state but employed by the county and the town, an extremely Virginian kind of arrangement. She looked out for the town's interests at the state level, and monitored state funds sent to help lift the town from the rut of poverty.

"Too independent by half," Connie said ruefully. "And success doesn't make you happy."

But Dawn wasn't through. "And now that you're assistant mayor, Momma says there's going to be some great things getting done."

"I got appointed because nobody else wanted the job."

"That's not true and you know it. You've already gotten a doctor to come to town. Isn't that a great start?"

Connie pulled up in front of Campbell's Grocery. She found it harder to let the child go on some days than others. Today it was like getting taffy off her teeth. "Is Duke bringing you home?"

"No, he's got some big meeting at the store."

"I have to go see Poppa Joe this afternoon. Mind coming with me?"

The young lady showed genuine delight. "Are you kidding?"

"I'm sorry about what I said, Dawn. I don't know what's kept me so riled."

"I do." She slid from the car, then said through the open door, "Momma always says I'm nine parts angel and one part migraine."

Connie drove off, waving at people she could hardly see for the sheen growing before her eyes. It was an old ache, one she had thought was long gone. But the sorrow held her still, murmuring right alongside the grumbling engine. There was too much truth in the old truck for her to refuse to see how much she wished Dawn had been her own child.

Connie drove from the grocery straight to the church. Before she could climb from the truck, Pastor Brian Blackstone came bounding down the stairs. Connie had known Brian since grade school, and the man looked as worried as she had ever seen him. When he opened the door to the truck, she greeted him with, "How is the baby?"

"Exactly the same." Hill country wisdom held that the best pastor was one who had suffered, so he could talk from experience when dealing with his flock. Brian Blackstone certainly fit that bill. "Don't tell me the doctor's decided not to come."

"Not as far as I know," Connie replied. "Why, have you heard something?"

"No, nothing. It's just that . . ." The pastor cast a worried glance around him. "I'm not certain this truck is the proper first impression we want to give our new doctor."

"Listen to you. 'Not certain we're giving a proper impression.'" She ground the clutch and levered the old truck into first. "You'd think you did your schooling at Harvard and not some Ozark college for hillbilly preachers."

"I attended seminary in Louisville, as you well know," Brian said stiffly. He glanced at his watch. "Are we late?"

"Calm down, Brian." Reverend Blackstone was from a Hillsboro family as old and set in Shenandoah country as her own. But somewhere along the way Brian had picked up a very proper way of talking. It hadn't come from seminary—Brian had spoken like this ever since grade school. It was only the fact that his big brother would have walloped anyone who made fun of Brian that had saved him from early torment. "We don't even know when he's arriving. All Fuller asked was for us to drop by the clinic and say our howdies."

"Then don't start just yet. Let's have a moment of prayer together." When she hesitated before cutting the motor, he insisted. "Connie, this new doctor could be absolutely crucial, to Sadie and to me and to the entire town."

"I know that." Still, she felt defensive. For the second time in one day someone had mentioned turning a problem over to the Lord. Connie cut off the engine and bowed her head. She listened as the pastor asked for success with their hopes of the day, and found herself growing increasingly nervous. Not over what lay ahead, but rather from what lay within. As soon as Brian announced the amen, she started the motor and pulled onto the road.

Brian gripped the dashboard as she took the corner onto Main. The front left suspension was going again, and the truck had a tendency to buck on curves. He asked, "How is Poppa Joe doing?"

"Still ornery over how they took away his driver's license." Connie's uncle was fast approaching his eighty-third birthday, and he tended to treat every road he met as his own. The last time the sheriff had stopped him, it was for mowing down a stop sign and carrying it until his busted radiator had given up the ghost. "Only way I knew to keep him from getting behind the wheel was to take the truck home with me."

"But why drive it today?"

"We're going out to see him this afternoon, Dawn and I." She drove down to where the street joined with the nicest bridge in town, one fashioned from granite so polished it reflected the morning sun like a water-born jewel. She took an easy right onto River Road and continued, "Driving his truck over reassures him that I'm keeping it up."

"I still think . . ." Brian's voice trailed off as she pulled into the weed-choked lot. Beneath the mass of greenery should have been a gravel parking area. "I thought they were going to regrade this."

"So did I." But Connie was far more concerned about how the clinic itself appeared. The fresh paint lay on the old structure like a new coat on a cadaver. "This place looks plain awful."

"We should have had it rebuilt long ago."

"Where were we supposed to find the money?" It was a litany so often expressed she didn't even have to think the words. They just came. Lack of funding defined her every action for the town she loved. "Don't worry, Brian. This doctor knows about our situation. We didn't paint him a rosy picture. No chance of that and be honest over why we haven't had a live-in doctor for almost three years."

It was not just the loss of their town's only doctor that caused hardship these days. But the problem typified what Connie and the rest of Hillsboro faced. Down below, the world had entered modern times. People worked at jobs that meant something. If they didn't like what they did, they walked out and went somewhere else and found another job. Flatland life was like that. But a good-paying job that gave a fellow a feeling of worth was often out of reach in the hills.

And it was not just work that separated them. Down below, the world was changing at a pace the hillfolk could hardly believe. People didn't just have more money in the flatlands, they had more things to buy. Televisions had appeared in most homes, if word could be believed. Up in the hills, those who had TV sets didn't watch them much because the snowy reception hurt their eyes and they could hardly hear what was being said.

Apparently the flatland world stopped dead in its tracks for shows like *Rawhide*, *The Ed Sullivan Show*, and *American Bandstand*. The newspapers were full of things that were little more than words on the page, like how a wall was being built down the middle of Berlin. And just this summer, President Kennedy himself had declared the goal of putting a man on the moon by the end of the decade. People would talk of such things and just shake their heads. It didn't hardly seem as though they were living in the same world any more.

Hillfolk liked to brag about going down the mountains and seeing such changes for themselves. When they returned home more often than not they declared stoutly that it didn't mean nothing but trouble to come. As though pessimism were the only defense the hillfolk had against hardship and isolation.

As Connie climbed down from the truck, she tugged at the front edges of her jacket, pretending to clear away the creases but in truth wishing she had worn something that did not make her look so thick. There were days when she could look in the mirror and see a woman who had retained her youthful energy and grace. Today, however, she had applied her makeup without really looking, fearing she would inspect herself and come up with a word like hefty. She hated mirrors on mornings like this.

Together with Brian she started across the unkempt lawn and listened for some sign of life. The clinic's front door was open, but the only sound came from the river chuckling from the ravine across the road. Brian asked, "Is my tie straight?"

"You look just fine." She gave him as reassuring a smile as she could manage. "I'm sure—"

From inside the clinic came the noise of a slamming door. A muffled voice said something, only to be answered with a shout of rage. Brian's nervous features creased with genuine worry. "That doesn't sound at all good."

"Maybe we'd better go lend Fuller a hand."

They climbed the concrete block stairs and entered the Hillsboro Clinic's reception area. The place had once been a mill worker's cottage, given to the state in lieu of unpaid taxes when the mill went bankrupt. That was back when the hill farmers stopped bringing their corn by horse cart to have it ground at the water-powered mill.

Not long afterward, a local fellow who had made it to medical school and then survived the First World War decided to return home. With the town's blessing he had turned the old mill house into a much-needed medical clinic.

But the local fellow had died three years earlier, after doctoring the mountain folk for almost forty years. By then, even the few friends who had managed to outlive him were admitting that the old man was long past his prime.

Even so, a doddering old curmudgeon a half-century away from medical school was far better than no doctor at all. As the town had come to know at its own cruel cost.

Connie and Brian entered the open door to find Mayor Fuller Allen standing in the middle of the front room. A sheen of perspiration turned his bald pate to a polished dome. "Doctor Reynolds, I'd be the first to admit the clinic is lacking a few things. But if you'd just—"

"A few things!" The dark-haired stranger swept an angry hand at the door leading to the examining rooms. "I've seen better-equipped high school labs!"

"But Doctor Reynolds—"

"And outhouses with a higher standard of cleanliness!" The doctor's gaze turned their way, and Connie found herself staring at gray eyes smoky with rage. "Are you my nurse?"

"Me?" She took an involuntary step back. "Goodness, no."

"Ida May called in sick," Fuller said miserably. "Of all days."

The angry gaze turned back to the mayor. "My nurse's name is Ida May?"

"She's very highly thought of," Connie said. Nervousness tumbled the words like they were caught in a wringer washer. "She runs the county health service, knows almost every family within thirty miles."

"How thrilling." The man was watching her as he would a rodent discovered in his operating theater. "Who are you?"

"This is Connie Wilkes," Fuller supplied. His normal bonhomie had been deflated like a punctured balloon. "Hillsboro's assistant mayor."

"My abject sympathies," he snapped. "Are you the one responsible for this nightmare of a clinic?"

"I guess I am." Connie drew herself up as well as she could. She had not expected this. Nothing like this.

It wasn't the man's anger that caught her so off guard. It was his looks. The doctor was more than simply handsome. He had the sharply defined authority of a very successful and intelligent man. His features were cut with surgical precision. A wide intellectual brow descended to the most penetrating gaze she had ever seen.

Connie struggled to gather herself, then said, "I told you in my letter how tough things have been for our community."

"Certainly. But this—" Another angry gesture at the back rooms. "This is an absolute farce!"

"You're right." There was nothing to be gained from glossing over the truth, she saw that now. "It's just horrible."

Her quiet agreement halted his ire, at least momentarily. Connie went on hurriedly, "The doctor whose place you're taking should have retired years ago. He got to the stage where he wouldn't let anyone touch a thing. After he died, we found records marked active for people who had died twenty years ago."

"But why—"

"Because there wasn't anybody else." It was Brian who spoke up. "We're desperate, Doctor Reynolds. I don't know how else to describe our situation. We're a proud people, and it costs us to have to admit it. But if we don't get a doctor in here soon, well, I just don't know what we'll do."

Nathan Reynolds eased back another notch. "And you are?"

"Brian Blackstone. I'm pastor of the local church."

"All right." The doctor had the ability to dominate a room by doing nothing more than crossing his arms. "I'm listening."

Brian took a breath. "The nearest hospital is sixty-four miles away, much of it over winding mountain roads. Our closest doctor is in Jonestown, that's thirty-eight miles. We're in the heart of the Appalachians here, and both towns are nightmare drives when the weather is bad. A lot of these local people simply won't make the journey. They don't trust doctors they don't know, and they have an inbred terror of hospitals. So they just lie in their beds and suffer. And then they die."

Connie found herself swallowing on sudden grief. The pain of Brian's role as pastor was there for all to see. She found herself adding, "Brian knows the road to Jonestown all too well. His baby's in a bad way."

A change came over the doctor. One so sudden it caught them all off guard. The arms uncrossed, the tone switched from rage to intense concern. "What's the problem?"

Brian glanced at Connie, uncertain what to say. "She's suffering in her stomach. She eats but can't keep anything down. And she seems to be in terrible pain."

Connie felt the same anxiety she always did when thinking of Brian and Sadie. She could not look at Brian or his wife, or watch him preach, or hear his name spoken, without thinking of the little child. The baby vomited convulsively and screamed constantly. She looked so weak and helpless and tired and pained that Connie could not stand to be near her, for fear of staring young death in the face.

The doctor gave a fraction of a nod. "Her age?"

"F-four months."

"You're sure it's not just an allergy?"

"She's allergic to her mother's milk, yes, but—"

"Does she spasm when she vomits?"

"Like her whole little body is twisting with pain," the pastor confirmed, aching with the words. "She can't keep anything down."

"You've tried different diets?"

"We went through a hard time finding a formula she could hold in even for a few minutes. The Jonestown doctor says she's allergic to almost everything."

Another sharp nod, like the firing pin coming down on an armed gun. "That happens with some infants. They probably put her on paregoric."

"Why, yes." Brian glanced Connie's way. "But it took the Jonestown doctor almost a month to come up with that one."

"And I suppose she went through a stable phase, except she was sleeping too much."

"We had to shake her hard just to keep her awake to eat."

"Then started regurgitating again?"

"Exactly." Brian swiped at his face. "She's gotten back to how she was before, and it's driving my wife crazy. We haven't had a decent night's sleep in six weeks. The baby just cries and—"

"Any secondary infections?"

"I don't . . . She keeps rubbing at her ears."

"That's normal." The words were cut and set with the precision of a machine running at blinding speed. "The child's resistance is low because she's not eating enough. Ears are a common center for viral infections in such cases."

Brian let his terror show through. "The Jonestown doctor says there's not much else we can do."

Connie could not help but add, "Brian's wife, Sadie, had a stillborn child three years ago, and since then they've had trouble conceiving. This has been harder on her than you can imagine."

The piercing gray gaze turned her way. The doctor studied her a long moment, then switched back to Brian. "Let me go see what I can find in this museum."

He turned and walked into the back. Connie felt as though a steel band had suddenly been released from around her chest.

Fuller Allen plucked a handkerchief from his back pocket. Owner of the town's only car dealership, he was a big florid man perfectly at home with chairing town meetings and glad-handing voters and kissing babies. Dealing with enraged doctors was another thing entirely. Quietly he asked Connie, "What do you know about this man?"

"Nothing more than what I've already told you." She could not get over the doctor's sheer intensity. "Up until about two years ago, he was assigned to a top hospital in Baltimore. Did his training in New York and someplace out west. Wrote a couple of articles on something, I couldn't even figure out the titles they sent me."

Connie looked from one man to the other, wondering if they felt the same way. As though they had been confronted with someone functioning on an entirely different level from themselves. "I called the last place he worked, a hospital in Baltimore. Spoke to some stuffy administrator. She basically said he was willing to come to Hillsboro and I'd be a fool not to take him. Acted like I didn't have any business asking more than that."

A muffled shout came through the open back door, followed by a crashing drawer and an enraged harangue. Fuller glanced over nervously, drew the handkerchief over his features a second time, and asked Connie, "How much do we have left in the town's discretionary fund?"

"Not a lot."

"Give him whatever he wants," Fuller said. "Within reason."

"What if—"

Connie halted at the sound of staccato footsteps coming back down the hallway. Nathan Reynolds stormed into the reception area and shouted at no one in particular, "This isn't a clinic, it's a gallery for medical nightmares!"

Brian stepped forward, and said one word. "Please."

Again there was that transformation, a shift from rage to fierce intensity. "All right. My car is packed to the gills, so you take another car. I need to take mine in case I need some instruments. I certainly didn't find anything of use back there!"

"I'll hang around and close up here," the mayor offered, relieved to have an excuse not to come.

The doctor was across the reception area and out the door before any of them had moved. Connie was next through the door, but in her haste she collided with him on the top step. "Oh, I'm sorry—"

He had been pushed down a step by her intrusion but kept his gaze on her truck. "That's a thirty-four Terraplane Pickup Express."

"Nineteen thirty-six, actually." She knew because her uncle had often used the truck's purchase date as a calendar. These days Poppa Joe felt like he was doing well to remember the right year. "But how do you—"

"Hudson didn't make that body style in nineteen thirty-six."

She found herself glad for a reason to contradict this superior attitude. "I'm sorry, but you're wrong."

"American trucks were my hobby as a kid. I know every model ever made." The doctor turned eyes of gray ice toward her, a gaze as cold as his voice. "That truck is a thirty-four model, not a thirty-six."

Then he was down and across the lot, almost sprinting for his car. "Don't just stand there! Let's go!"

Connie fumed her way to Reverend Brian Blackstone's house, coming up with a dozen or so smart things to put the doctor in his place. Then she noticed the pastor smiling at her. "What're you grinning at?"

"You've got your face all screwed up." He made a parody of somebody mouthing off in silence. "I haven't seen you do that since you were a kid and mad at Poppa Joe."

"That's the silliest thing I ever heard."

"Sister, every time you returned from a visit to his place you'd steam up the school bus windows with your rage. You'd sit there and argue with the old coot the entire way into town. We used to have competitions out in the schoolyard, seeing who could come closest to your crazy faces."

"I never understood why some churches moved their preachers around every few years," Connie retorted hotly. "Until just this minute."

His grin broadened another notch. "The doc got under your skin back there, didn't he?"

"It's not gonna be long before somebody carves their initials in the belt of Doctor Fancy-Pants," she predicted.

"I don't know if you're right about that. These hills are full of people bent on walking God's road their own ornery way." He waited until she had swung wide around the church and started down the road leading to his home. "You mark my words. A lot of our folk will put more weight on his being the kind of man who's rushing to see my baby after driving hundreds of miles, even before he's unpacked his car."

Brian glanced around to make sure the doctor's car was still stuck to their tail, then turned his smile back to her and went on. "You think people around here are going to mind that he's got the personality of an angry porcupine?"

But Connie wasn't ready to let go of her perfectly good mad just yet. "I hope he doctors as good as he barks, is all I'm saying."

The doctor was out of his car and fumbling in the back seat before they had climbed from the truck. He pulled out what looked like a case of medical samples and started rummaging. Soon the ground around his car was littered with vials and prospectuses and brochures. Angrily he kicked the box aside, dived back in the car, pulled out a second case, and continued searching. Finally he rose, one hand full of little boxes. "All right, let's go."

The mountain preacher said, "I can't thank you enough—"

"Save it." Nathan Reynolds shut the door and went around to the passenger seat. He pulled out the battered black bag that had belonged to the old doctor. Seeing the dusty satchel brought to Connie a pang of memories. But it only seemed to enrage the doctor further. He slammed the door and snapped at her, "I'll be giving you a list of medical supplies I expect you to buy tonight, even if it means driving all the way to Richmond!"

She had a lifetime's experience of dealing with bad tempers. "You do, and I'll roll it up and stick it straight in your eye!"

Brian's expression turned worried. "Connie, please."

Before the doctor could snap out a response, the pastor's front door opened, and a woman's voice said, "You're going to have to take your quarrels somewhere else. I've just gotten the baby to sleep."

An instantly contrite Connie turned from the confrontation and walked over to the front porch. "Hello, Sadie. I'm sorry. How are you?"

"Tired." She did not look tired. She looked exhausted. She was a small-boned woman, ten years younger than the pastor, and normally full of life and determination. But the past four months had aged her.

Sadie looked over Connie's shoulder, took in the cases and the leather bag, and surmised, "Are you the doctor?"

He gave a nod as sharp as his tone. "Nathan Reynolds."

"Well, praise the Lord," she said, though there was little energy there for thanks. "Come in. Please."

He bounded up the porch stairs, pressing Connie into moving and thinking at a faster pace. As they entered the house, a faint mewing started in the back room. Sadie said tiredly, "I don't suppose it matters that she's woken up again."

"No," Nathan Reynolds agreed, his tone subdued for the first time that day. He entered the nursery and spent a long moment staring down at the crib. "Tell me about her sleeping habits."

"Like you see." Fatigue had turned Sadie's speech as staccato as the doctor's. "Exhaustion knocks her out, pain wakes her up. She frets and cries until she doesn't have any more energy, then she sleeps until her tummy wakes her up again."

"And her eating?"

"She's so hungry." Sadie choked back a sob. "The poor little thing. These past few days she starts crying when I show her the bottle. She's starving, but she knows if she eats she's going to hurt even worse."

Connie found herself stiffening as the doctor bent over the crib. But the touch he used in lifting the little baby was as gentle as his manner was rough. "I'd like to see her eat, please."

"She'll get it all over you."

"That's all right."

Brian offered, "I'll go warm up the bottle."

Nathan Reynolds asked Sadie, "Are you trying to hold to any sort of schedule?"

"How can I?" She brushed at a wisp of hair with the manner of a woman twice her age. "She's up and crying every hour or so. I feed her as much as she'll take, she holds it in for about ten minutes, then throws it all back up again."

"All right, here's what I want us to do." Somehow his hands and his voice seemed untouched by the fussing baby. Not only that, but they seemed to be calming the mother. "Take one of these boxes here and mix the powder with one-half cup of water."

Hesitantly Sadie accepted the box, read the label, "Maalox?"

"It's a new drug they've developed for ulcers in adults. Setting standards in hospital trials. We've seen some good results in treating babies with pyloric stenosis."

"Here, I'll do that," Connie offered, and slipped the box from Sadie's hand.

As she moved to the kitchen she heard the tired woman say, "What was that you just said?"

"Pyloric stenosis. Typical cause of infant spasm after eating." The doctor's tone was as softly gentle now as it had been angry before. Willing the woman to calm, to strengthen, to hope. "Naming a problem is not solving it, but as I've said, Maalox has shown good results in some cases."

When Connie returned, he accepted the glass without raising his eyes from the baby. "All right. Let's start with a dosage of two milligrams. Bring me a teaspoon."

"But the doctor said—"

"What the doctor told you is not working, is it?" When his words quietened Sadie Blackstone, he went back to examining the baby. Long supple fingers touched and probed, but in ways that did not seem to fret the baby any more than she already was. Which was remarkable, as the child normally did not like to be touched by anyone but her mother. Not even Brian.

"I also want to put her on antibiotic drops for her ears." His gaze rose to Connie, but this time there was no animosity. "Is there a pharmacy in town?"

"Yes."

"Call them and see if they stock tetracycline drops. If not, ask them for a substitute."

Brian announced from the kitchen, "The formula is ready."

"Fine." Nathan dropped his eyes back to the baby. "Why don't we give her the first dosage now before she eats."

The room seemed quietly galvanized. Sadie moved to the cupboard, Connie to the phone. She dialed the pharmacy number from memory and listened to it ring as Brian brought in the bottle.

A languid voice said, "Sedrick's."

"Phil, it's Connie Wilkes."

"Hey, gal. That doctor fellow showed up yet?"

"Yes." Phil Sedrick sat on the town council with her. He was a slow-moving mountain man who had inherited the pharmacy and his mother's easy manner but not his father's intelligence. Connie asked, "Is the pharmacist on duty?"

"Naw, she's gone to lunch. It's just me holding down the fort. What can I do you for?"

She spelled out the drops. "See if you have them or an equivalent in stock. Call me back at Brian's as soon as you know."

"Suppose I could give a look-see down back. But say—"

"I have to go. Do it fast, please. Immediately." She hung up before he could start on one of his rambling conversations.

Connie stood there at the back of the room, watching the doctor speak in soothing tones as he forced the baby to take what clearly was a very unappetizing medicine. He did not flinch as she blew the first mouthful back into his face. Nor did he mind as she cried and fretted after swallowing the second try, or when she threw up half the bottle of formula down his shirt front. He simply held her and observed. His intensity of concentration was almost frightening.

When the baby started to fall asleep, the doctor surprised them all by shaking the little girl back awake. "Let's try it again now."

"But won't—"

"Let me have the bottle again." Though the tone was mild for the baby's sake, the imperious manner was still there in full force. "Now."

Doubtfully Sadie Blackstone handed it back, and watched as he inserted the nipple and kept gently shaking the baby, forcing her to waken and suckle. To everyone's astonishment, she did so without apparent discomfort.

Even the baby's eyes opened in surprise. Two little fists came up to curl around the bottle.

Nathan Reynolds stopped shaking her, and sat there holding her and allowing her to take as much as she wanted. "Maalox has a very sticky consistency, specifically meant to keep it from being thrown back up. Her tummy is coated now, so this batch ought to stay down."

Sadie bent over, ran a finger down the side of her baby's face. "This is a miracle."

"We'll have to monitor her closely. Her weight should begin to pick up, and when it does, her dosage will need to be adjusted. I'll need to weigh her every few days for the next three to four weeks. Can you bring her by the clinic?"

"Of course." A single tear coursed down the side of Sadie's face. She swallowed the shakiness in her voice and said, "What time?"

"I have no idea. Let's just play this by ear until I get settled."

He handed over the baby, used the washcloth Brian offered to wipe the worst of the formula from his shirt, then started for the door. "Until tomorrow."

Nathan Reynolds was out the door so fast the only mark of Sadie's gratitude was an unseen hand raised to the space he had just left behind.

Brian hastened after him, and Connie followed. The doctor was halfway across the yard toward his car before the scampering pastor caught up. "Doctor Reynolds!"

Reluctantly the man turned back, the hostile chill clear in his eyes.

In his quiet manner, Brian asked, "If you hadn't been here, could my baby have died?"

"It depends on her constitution. Babies are stronger than they look." Clearly he knew where this conversation was headed. Even so, he reluctantly agreed. "But yes, it is a distinct possibility."

Brian nodded slowly, hollowed by the news and how close they had come to another nightmare. All he said was, "Then you see our town's desperate need."

Nathan Reynolds seemed exasperated by the discussion. He opened his mouth, snapped it shut, and searched the yard with angry eyes. Then his gaze fastened upon Connie's truck. He swiveled back to glare at her and assert, "Allowing a vehicle like that to deteriorate is an absolute crime. But having seen the state of your clinic, I guess I shouldn't be surprised."

Before she could recover and form the words boiling up with her ire, he had stomped to his car. Nathan Reynolds departed in a cloud of angry dust and scattered gravel.

Sadie Blackstone stepped up beside her, and said quietly, "A miracle."

Four

When Connie pulled up in front of the grocery that afternoon, she found Dawn waiting with her mother. Hattie Campbell opened the door and asked, "Mind if I come along?"

"Hop on in."

"I haven't seen Poppa Joe in weeks." Hattie lifted three big sacks of groceries into the back, then climbed in after her daughter and demanded, "So how's the new fellow?"

"He's a doctor to his bones." Connie had already decided that a diplomatic approach was required for such queries. Let the town find out for themselves. If he stayed around. "A one hundred percent, pure-bred, citified doctor."

"That bad, huh?" But Hattie was smiling. And her smile was what she shared most with her daughter. That and their love of life. "I heard there was a little set-to in the clinic this morning."

Connie had to slow the truck and stare. Dawn let go with a giggle.

"Not to mention a little miracle-working over at Reverend Blackstone's place," Hattie went on.

“I am constantly amazed,” Connie declared. “Not even light can travel as fast as a rumor in this town.”

Hattie settled back, satisfied. Her reddish brown hair was two shades darker than Connie’s and cut very short, making her jawline appear even sharper than it was. Her nose was narrow and long, her lips a quick red slit pressed constantly into a half-formed smile. Her brown eyes had the penetrating stare of one amply bestowed with common sense.

She could not have looked any more different from her daughter. Hattie Campbell had the high cheekbones and warm skin tones that suggested a touch of Indian blood. When Hattie was growing up, this had been a mark of shame. The unmistakable taint had deepened her already quiet nature. Hattie was a reserved woman with all save those she knew and trusted. With friends, however, her quick wit and happy nature bubbled forth. Connie had considered Hattie Campbell a treasure since early childhood. One so precious that not even having Hattie land her man could shatter their closeness.

Dawn asked, “Is he really going to make that Blackstone baby stop wailing?”

“He might,” Connie allowed. “He might at that.”

“So he’s a good doctor and a bad person,” Hattie offered from her side of truck.

“He’s got all the charm of a skunk,” Connie agreed.

“A skunk with a bellyache. Somebody who smells bad and acts worse,” Dawn chimed in. “That’s what Poppa Joe would say.”

“Now there’s a thought,” Hattie said. “Maybe you ought to bring those two together.”

“Not a chance,” Connie replied. But in truth she was caught by the idea, for reasons she could not fathom. “It took almost three years to get us a doctor. I don’t want to lose him the first afternoon.”

Conversation was cut off by their leaving the rural road for the long rutted track leading up to Wilkes Mountain.

That was its real name, though it wasn’t much in the way of a real mountain. There had once been a time when the early Wilkes settlers had held claim to much of the valley. They had been among the first pioneers to track this far down the Shenandoah Valley and had set claim to a long stretch of river-bottom farmland and as much of the surrounding hills as they could walk in three days. But hard times and spendthrift generations had reduced the holdings to scrubland and hillside that was of little use to anyone else.

The track rose like a country roller coaster, growing steadily steeper until they were pressed as much back as down into the old squeaking seats. Connie ground into first gear and floored the accelerator. The motor roared in welcome to its home for nigh on a quarter of a century. The truck had climbed this mile-long track in every kind of weather, and seemed to find its own way over the dips and ruts and rain-washed stones.

They swooped over a ridge invisible from the road below and entered an eighty-acre saddle-back. At the far end, nestled among the aspen and highland firs, stood a log cabin.

Three tumbledown corrals sectioned off much of this highland meadow, evidence of a time when Poppa Joe used to herd some cattle. A finger of smoke rose from a chimney made of creek-bed stones. It was the same welcome-home signal Connie had known since her parents had died in a traffic accident two days before her sixteenth birthday.

But the tall mountain man did not appear on the porch to greet them. Poppa Joe Wilkes liked to say that he could hear somebody coming a good ten minutes before he saw them, and this from a man who could shoot a flipped coin from the air at thirty paces. Connie had seen him do it.

"Maybe he's asleep," Dawn said doubtfully.

"Poppa Joe lie down while the sun's up?" Hattie squinted through the front windshield. "Not unless he's laid out by the man in black."

"Momma, hush your talk." But Dawn was worried too. "You think maybe he's off fishing?"

"Not with a fire going. Maybe . . ." Connie was silenced by man stepping out of the porch shadows. He wore a brown uniform and a broad brown hat.

Hattie moaned. "Oh, no. Not again."

But Dawn was delighted. "Oh, I hope it's turkey. I was thinking about roasted wild turkey all morning."

Connie said nothing. She pressed down harder on the accelerator. The old truck scooted and jounced over the roughshod track, tossing them around. Connie did not slow until they entered the dusty front yard. She scattered gravel and chickens as she came to a shuddering halt. The motor

coughed and rattled and died, satisfied to be back where it belonged.

Then all three spotted the second thread of smoke, this one rising from the half-buried little house set up inside the first line of trees.

"Oh, Poppa Joe, don't tell me," Connie moaned.

"Come on, Dawn, let's go inside the cabin, honey," Hattie said, climbing from the truck.

For once her daughter did not respond with sass. They slipped by the officer as he descended the sagging front steps, and disappeared into the shadows.

Slowly Connie approached the ranger. The man was unknown to her, which made it even worse. "Afternoon, officer."

"Ma'am." He touched the tip of his hat. "Are you a relation of Mr. Joseph Wilkes?"

"It's pronounced *Wilkies*," she corrected. "We've held to the old English way. Call it mule-headed stubbornness." She offered a tentative smile. When the young ranger remained stony-faced, she gave an inward sigh. She knew this kind of forest ranger all too well. "Yessir. Poppa Joe is my uncle."

"Ma'am, your uncle has been hunting deer out of season."

She crossed her arms in self-defense. "I take it you didn't actually see him shoot the animal."

The tough tone caught him off guard. "Ma'am?"

"If you had, we wouldn't be standing here talking, now, would we? What happened is, you were patrolling the parkland border, and you smelled his smokehouse."

The young man was blond and strong jawed and had the accent of somebody born a thousand miles from these hills. "Ma'am, there are fresh deer haunches dressed and hanging in that smokehouse."

And venison sausages too, if she knew Poppa Joe. But Connie chose not to say that. "Officer . . . What's your name, please?"

"Harding."

"Officer Harding, I've talked to the old man until I'm blue in the face. If you want him to stop hunting out of season, you're just going to have to do it yourself."

Again there was the sense of not hearing what he had expected. "Ma'am, your uncle tells me he's never carried a hunting license. Hunting out of season and not having a license both carry thousand-dollar fines."

Connie knew this type. The Shenandoah National Forest, one of the country's poorest parklands, was used as a testing ground for too many young rangers. Men and women alike, they arrived fresh-faced and full of ideals instilled at universities in Boulder or Boston or Seattle. Big-city college graduates, who sat in classrooms and learned about a perfect world, and spent their weekends hiking places like Yellowstone or Yosemite or the Appalachian Trail. Nothing in their books and lessons ever brought them close to somebody like Poppa Joe Wilkes.

This particular young ranger was caught up in having treed his first two-legged prey. He held to his stern, straight-eyed line and went on, "Not only that, ma'am, but there's every evidence that he shot that deer on national parkland. That's a felony, punishable by a year in prison."

"Now you look here!" Connie uncrossed her arms and took a menacing step toward the ranger. The fire was burning in her now. The same fire that had been started by the doctor that morning and never given a chance to flare. "If you don't stop with this nonsense, I'm going inside for Poppa Joe's gun and end your career before it gets started!"

He took a half-step away from her. "Ma'am—"

"One glance at that peach fuzz on your chin is enough to tell me this is your first assignment," she snapped. "When did you get out of school, last May?"

Connie's anger was legendary. It had been born from the rage and frustration of losing her parents too early, and fueled by feeling her life had never returned to its proper track. She used it on lazy road crews and recalcitrant state finance officers and everybody in between. The townsfolk called her Surefire Wilkes behind her back, took pride in how she got things done, and made it a point to stay out of her way when her eyes were flashing fire.

Like now. "I never did understand why the Park Service figured on us having to give you boys the decent education you should've gotten in school."

"Now wait—"

"You just hush up and listen." She turned and swung her arm in a broad arc. "Our property abuts the park right along that ridgeline to the southern border. You hear what I'm saying?"

Connie watched that bit of news register on his unlined face. He risked a single glance back toward the ramshackle cabin. "You're telling me that man in there—"

"Owns nigh on seventeen hundred acres. It's mostly rock and scrub and land too steep for anybody but mountain goats and deer. But it's *our land.* Anybody who's spent ten *days* in these hills knows Poppa Joe would never cross into national parkland after a deer. Why? Because he doesn't need to."

She knew her accent was thickening and couldn't have cared less. "This land's been in our family since before the Revolutionary War. Is this getting through that thick wad of cotton wool you're wearing under your hat? We were here a hundred years before they ever even *thought* of making a park service so's to give you wide-eyed innocents something to do with our tax dollars."

It cost him, she could see it in his eyes, but he managed to hold his ground. "Ma'am, if your uncle doesn't stop hunting out of season, I'm going to have to arrest him."

As swiftly as the anger had risen, it evaporated. It often happened that way, and when it left her, it left her empty. Connie said, "Poppa Joe Wilkes is the last of a dying breed. He's forgotten more about these hills than you'll ever learn."

"Even so—"

"Look here. Before you do something rash, why don't you go talk to some of the people down in Hillsboro. Or better still, see if you can find a ranger who's been around a while. Ask them how you'll seem, trying to lock this old man up."

She could see him falter, realizing he had opened a can

of worms, and she felt awash in shame for her own anger. "I buy a hunting license for Poppa Joe every year. He just refuses to carry it." Again there was no reaction from the young man, but she pressed on. "Tell you what. Why don't you step inside, talk to my uncle about the hills. You'd be amazed what you can learn from him. His great-granddaddy even hunted these parts with Daniel Boone, did you know that?"

"No, ma'am." He remained stiff and unbending. "I didn't, and it doesn't matter."

"Better still, come have a plate with us." She tried for a smile. "Bet you've never had smoked venison with grits and collards."

"I'll be going now, ma'am." He touched the rim of his hat a second time. "Somebody'll be coming by with a truck this evening to collect the evidence."

She stood and watched him march back into the woods. There was a ranger trail about a quarter-mile further up the ridge where he'd probably parked his truck. And a well-worn path down to Poppa Joe's. Some rangers came to arrest him, others came to learn. But sooner or later, they all came. She had a feeling about this one, though. He would go back and make his report and feel shamed by the older officers laughing at him. And he would never come back, leaving both him and the old man poorer from his absence. All because she could not hold fast to her temper.

When the ranger had vanished inside the trees and their lengthening shadows, Connie sighed herself around and started toward the cabin.

Five

Connie climbed the front steps, crossed the porch, and pushed open the door on its creaky leather hinges. She stared at the tall old man in the far corner and declared, "I just went and wasted a perfectly good mad on that poor boy, when I should have come in here and used it on you."

"Had me a hankering for deer." But Poppa Joe's familiar bluster wasn't there. "Not a thing in the world the matter with wanting some fresh game."

"There is too and you know it." Connie watched as he carried his metal plate over to the deep granite sink. The old man's movements had become so shaky that the fork and knife clattered on the edge. The sound was a chattering worry to her heart. "They're gonna put you in jail if you don't stop."

"Every single thing I shoot I eat. That oughtta count for something in this mixed-up world." His hand shook so hard he had to brush his fingers across the pump handle before getting a grip and beginning to heave up and down. Water spouted and poured into the sink. "Any of you ladies like a cup of cold well-water?"

"I would, Poppa Joe." Dawn walked over and took a metal cup off its hook on the wall. With her other hand she offered him a slender package. "I brought you something."

"Girl, you shouldn't oughtta done that." He filled her cup, stopped pumping, and accepted the packet of five cigars. "White Owls. Nice how you remember them's my favorites."

"But a deer, Poppa Joe." Connie's protest grew feebler as she watched him cross the cabin in hesitant steps. "You know how these new rangers are about deer out of season."

"All I know is, the foals is dropped, the antlers is high, and the weather's turning. That makes it deer season in my book."

Poppa Joe stepped onto the porch, unwrapped one of the cigars and said to Dawn, "Light me a taper, honey."

"Here." Hattie Campbell entered the golden light of dusk carrying a twig lit from the stove. "Connie's right, you know. They really will put you in jail."

He took his time getting the cigar lit and drawing well, then lowered himself into the rocker. "I just wanted me one last deer. And that's all the truth there is to tell."

Connie eased herself down on the top step and leaned against the railing. The words left her heart chilled, as though they contained a warning she was not yet ready to decipher.

Sunsets were much longer affairs than in the valley below. The saddle-back faced a low-slung pass, one which caught and nestled the sun for hours on hot summer evenings. The cabin was built up snug to the saddle-back's steep northern rise, protected from stiff winter winds. The meadow stretched out before her like a soft golden sea.

The last of autumn thistle floated in the breathless air, and the smell of late wildflowers and honeysuckle and sweet untilled earth filled Connie's senses. Seated on the top step and leaning on the railing had been her favorite spot since she was little. Connie sat and listened as Hattie and Dawn talked about the new doctor, and felt overwhelmed with worry about a world without Poppa Joe.

She was finally drawn around by her uncle leaning down and saying, "I don't hold with folks ignoring me on my front porch, daughter."

"And I don't hold with having to bail you out of trouble every time I come up here." But the response lacked the snap to work through his thick skin.

"I was telling you to invite the doctor up here for a visit."

"I'm not sure that's a good idea."

"Look here, daughter. You want the doctor fellow to stay, now, don't you?"

"Yes, and that's exactly—"

"Well, it ain't gonna be the town that'll keep him here." Poppa Joe sat and puffed on his cigar, the cigar smoke ringing his head like a gray wreath. "Now you just think on that for a country minute."

Six

The Reverend Brian Blackstone found it hard to climb the clinic steps. Which was strange, seeing as how he and his wife had done so every third day for the previous six weeks. But this visit was different. This time he was coming as a pastor and not as a patient. And he found himself fearing the man inside.

Doctor Nathan Reynolds was gaining himself quite a reputation. First of all, he refused all social contact. Entirely. He had not even attended the Elks banquet held in his honor. The previous week, when the mayor had tried to have him sit at the podium table so the town could publicly thank him on Founder's Day, Nathan Reynolds had refused point-blank. When the embarrassed mayor had tried to insist, the doctor had threatened to pack up and depart.

He had also succeeded in driving off Ida May, his nurse and receptionist, after just one morning of working together. He would have been utterly alone in the clinic, had Hattie Campbell not offered to help out. Hattie had trained as a nurse but never worked as one, having joined her husband in the grocery right after school. According to patients who had spoken about it to Brian, Hattie's lack of experience was a constant source of outbursts.

According to rumor, Connie Wilkes had also come by twice to extend an invitation to visit Poppa Joe up on Wilkes Mountain, a proposal that would have had anybody else in the valley jumping for their hat. But Nathan Reynolds had blasted Connie out the door both times.

He refused to say how long he was staying. If he met a patient on the street, he simply turned away.

Nathan Reynolds was rude and sharp and perpetually angry. He viewed the world through a bitter squint. He was acrid in his tone and nasty in his speech. He did everything possible to push people away. No doubt about it, Doctor Nathan Reynolds was one severely cantankerous individual.

As Brian Blackstone entered the clinic's waiting room, he reflected that he had never seen the makings of a more lonely man.

Hattie smiled as he pushed through the door. "Brian, hello, don't tell me the baby's acting up again."

"The baby's fine." He nodded to the people crowding the room's tattered furniture. The place had a musty, faded air.

The only bright spot was the smile on Hattie's face. Brian seated himself on the little chair by her desk and asked quietly, "How are you holding out?"

"All right." But the smile was forced, the tone quieter. The other people pretended not to listen. "Since it's you who's asking, I'll admit to the fact that the man in there scares me silly."

"Should we try to find somebody to replace you?"

"No, no, it'd probably be some near child who's never had to deal with an angry customer. At least that's one lesson I've gotten down pat." She cast a swift glance back toward the closed door. "Ten minutes with him on a bad day, and you'd be out looking for another assistant."

"I suppose that's true."

"Besides, you know how quiet it is around the grocery this time of year. We could use the extra income."

Brian glanced behind him. There was not a free seat. And two men stood in the far corners, talking in low tones to their seated wives. "Certainly does look busy."

"A lot of these folks have been storing up their ailments for quite a while. Since nobody knows how long he's here for, they're getting in while the getting's good." Hattie rose to her feet. "Let me go see if Doctor Reynolds'll take a couple of minutes and speak with you."

Brian made his way around the room, greeting each person in turn. He had long since come to know most of the residents in the Hillsboro region, even those traveling in from neighboring valleys and distant highland farms. He talked weather and crops and relatives, just letting them know he was there and caring.

"Brian?" When he turned, he found Hattie's smile had become even more forced. "He'll see you now."

When he passed her, she pointed to the far corner door and murmured, "You might want to make it brief."

Brian followed her directions, knocked on the open door, and said, "Afternoon, Nathan."

The doctor did not look up from his desk. He snapped at the paper he was writing on. "I can't believe I'm expected to write out my own records. Haven't you people ever heard of electric typewriters and secretaries who take shorthand?"

"Yes." Brian walked over and seated himself. And waited. He was good at that. He had met and disarmed a lot of anger simply by accepting whatever came.

Finally the doctor raised his gaze. "You feeling ill?"

"No, I'm fine, thank you."

"Sadie all right? The baby?"

"They're both doing well. I can't thank you enough—"

"Then don't even start." Nathan Reynolds bent back over his desk, his face hidden behind strands of dark hair going prematurely gray.

Brian sat where he was. There were a few moments in his life when he felt the Spirit move in a most intimate fashion. There was no sense of voices or words or a hand guiding him. Instead there sometimes came a silent sensation of a door opening, an unseen opportunity. A tiny crack through which he could insert a word. If only he were very careful, very watchful, very alert.

So he sat where he was, and he examined this antagonistic man before him. And he waited.

Eventually the pen stopped scratching, and the eyes peered in hostile closure. "You still here?"

"Yes. Still right here." That was another fact of such times. Nothing said or done could faze him. Perhaps it was because he was too concerned with hearing what was inaudible, just beyond his earthly reach. "I was just wondering . . ."

"I've got a thousand things more important than your wonderings." The voice was flat, final. "Stop wasting my time."

"Don't you ever need anybody?" Brian had no idea where the words came from. But he couldn't take them back, so there was no need to try. "Don't you ever—"

"Look." Angrily the doctor slapped the file closed. "I know where this is headed, and it's not going to work."

Amazing. The miracle was happening again. "Where am I headed, Nathan?"

"To God. Am I right? You're going to sit there and you're going to lay the God jabber on me."

"Only if you want me to."

"Well, I don't." The doctor slammed another file open before him. "So back off."

The barrier against Nathan's ire remained complete. "What's got you so angry?"

"Death." The word was a bark. The sound punched out. "That clear enough for you?"

"Yes. I hate it too."

"Fine. So the subject is closed, all right?" The head dropped back down again. But not before Brian saw Nathan's face age to a mask of ancient fatigue. The man carried a burden that made Brian's heart ache and his mind wonder.

The pen scratched, the silence lingered, until the muttered words emerged, "You're just waiting to pounce, aren't you? Trying to find some way of telling me that everything's just fine. That there's nothing wrong with death since we're all headed for heaven or glory or some utter nonsense."

"I wasn't going to say anything like that."

He might as well not have spoken. "Let me ask you one thing, preacher man. What would you say if it wasn't some stranger off the street who was doing the dying, but your own little girl? You think you could sit there and be so rational, tell me how great it is because she's not suffering any more?"

"No." Brian did not feel the anger, nor the attack, nor the stabbing fury behind the words. The same words that left the doctor's hand shaking so hard he held the pen poised over the file, unable to write any longer. Here at this moment he was even protected from the keening memory of their first stillborn baby. His voice laced with a calm not his own, Brian said, "No, I wouldn't think that at all."

"What do you know. An honest preacher." The words were laced with bitter ridicule. "Wish you'd been around where I used to work."

"Tell me about your work, Nathan."

"No." Another bark. The pen was tossed aside. "This isn't one of your confessional hours. I didn't sign on for counseling."

"All right." Brian rose to his feet. Strange how he could feel satisfied when he had accomplished nothing but to irritate the man who was saving his daughter's life. "You know, I'd be honored to talk with you sometime. It isn't often I have the chance to lock horns with a man of your intelligence."

The face lifted once more. The voice remained bitter, but Nathan's gaze took on a look of wounded ire. "Yeah? Think some of your fancy words might change my mind about death?"

"No, I wasn't going to talk about death at all." He smiled down at the man, knowing the love he was feeling was not his own. "I was thinking maybe you might like to talk about life."

Nathan Reynolds stormed through the remainder of his day, vowing that it would be his last in this forsaken hole of a town. Yet the faces and the unspoken pleas refused to let his heart agree with what his mind kept repeating.

He left the clinic and walked back to the house given to him by the town. On the way, he started a mental list of everything he needed to do to get himself ready to return to the city and his work. *Real* work.

All afternoon he had struggled to hold on to the ire raised by the pastor. Anger was the perfect fuel to get him out of town. Rage had been his best defense against the assaults of the past two years. When all else had deserted him—friends and energy and time and reason—his fury had still been there. He had fought his way through the pain and the misery, and he had survived. But now, in the face of these strange people and their even stranger ways, his anger was somehow not working as it should. He could not even stay irritated at the pastor. And that rankled most of all.

Nathan's heart and half his mind remained held by the faces of the patients he had seen that day. Their quiet acceptance of pains and illnesses baffled him. And their gratitude, that was another mystery. He found himself searching for a way to describe the manner with which they met his ire and his harshness. When he fastened upon the word, it stopped him there in the middle of the street. They treated him with *homage*. They *honored* him.

He forced his feet to move on. The Shenandoah River ran alongside the road he walked back to his home. His temporary home, he corrected himself, as he tried to shake off the thoughts and focus on getting ready to leave. But the river seemed to be chuckling at him and his attempts to stay angry. Mocking him and his plans and his rage.

Just as he started down his drive, the sound of a roaring engine and squealing tires brought him back around. A truck took the turning into River Road on two wheels. He could see the driver scramble the wheel around and aim straight for where Nathan was standing.

The truck skidded to a halt. Through the windshield Nathan spotted two smaller figures seated beside the driver. Both of the children were wailing.

Nathan was about to shout at the driver for having scared the children with his driving, when the man leaped clear of the truck and called hoarsely, "You the doc?"

"Nathan Reynolds. What—"

"Praise the Lord." The man scrambled around the truck on worn rubber galoshes. He looked like a scrawny throwback to frontier days, with a long dark beard and hair tumbling all over his shoulders. Yet this particular man wore a sopping wet nightshirt and a torn hunting jacket. As he drew closer Nathan realized the man still had soap suds in his hair. "Name's Will Green. I farm a piece over Humbolt Mountain way."

Nathan found his arm gripped by a hand as tight as an iron vise. "You mind letting—"

"It's my wife, Doc. She ain't breathing right."

He found himself running through the standard ops list as the man marched him toward the truck. "She have a history of asthma?"

"Naw, she's allus been right healthy."

"Chest infections? Sudden pains?"

The man pulled him around the side. Suddenly a sound of choking became audible. "You can ask her yourself, Doc. I done flung a mattress in the back and carted her down."

Seven

Friday Connie drove to the clinic in a foul mood. Word had come down from Richmond of new budget cuts. Small mountain towns were the first to be hit when times got hard, since they lacked the political clout to protect themselves. Connie had spent five hours pleading and cajoling to keep their meager city-works budget intact, and still felt uncertain as to meeting their future needs.

To make matters worse, over Thanksgiving dinner Poppa Joe had again pestered her to bring the doctor up for a visit. In his quiet, stubborn way he had finally worn her down. As much as she despised having anything further to do with the doctor, she had agreed to extend Nathan Reynolds one final invitation.

Ever since the doctor's arrival six weeks earlier, she had been hearing reports. Her own two visits had been brief and explosive, his reaction to her earlier invitations acerbic. She thus took quiet satisfaction from how the townspeople used Nathan Reynolds but otherwise steered clear of his cantankerous ways. All but Hattie; for some unexplained reason, she had continued with the duties of receptionist. Hattie claimed it was because they needed the money. But Connie felt her oldest friend was telling only half the truth, and she could not understand why.

As Connie pulled up in front of the clinic, she spotted a familiar face. Will Green dropped the box he was carrying in the back of his truck and waved in her direction. The Greens' homestead was one of the valley's fringe farmlands. Connie waved back at Will and recalled hearing how the doctor had recently saved his wife's life with an emergency operation. Something about her breathing.

Connie climbed from her car and walked over, but she did not offer her hand. Many of the traditional mountain folk didn't take to shaking a single woman's hand, unless it was on a hoedown floor. "How are you, Will?"

"Howdy, Miss Connie. Doing just fine, thankee."

"And your wife?"

"She's makin' steady progress, thanks to the Lord and Doc Reynolds." He tossed a glance over his shoulder. "You heard anything 'bout whether the doc'll be staying?"

"Not yet." She studied his truck, which was crammed

full of boxes and strange metal apparatus. "What are you doing here?"

"Oh, me and some of the boys, we said we'd help him with—"

"Will!" The clinic's door slammed back on its hinges. "I thought I told you to get those boxes and the rest of that junk out of the front two rooms!"

"Just gettin' on it, Doc."

"Well, it doesn't look like it to me!" Nathan Reynolds stomped down the three concrete steps. "The place is still packed to the gills, and you're standing around here yapping! And what about those friends of yours?"

Will Green was the kind of man who had never made a passing acquaintance with fury. Connie knew a number of such strong gentle men from hillside families, and it rankled mightily to watch the farmer peel the hat from his head and begin spinning it nervously with work-scarred hands. "They'll be here directly, Doc. They promised soon as they were done up to—"

"Soon is not good enough," the man raged. He turned at the sound of footsteps scraping over the newly regraded gravel parking area. Hattie scurried over and gave him a decidedly nervous smile. He lashed out, "And you are twenty minutes late!"

She cringed under his blazing ire. "Sorry, Doctor Reynolds, we had a late delivery at the store and Chad—"

"I don't want excuses, I want some discipline around this

place! We've got a full waiting room and I'm in there by myself!" He wheeled back to the cowed farmer and shouted, "You and your lazy good-for-nothing—"

Connie felt something snap in her head. "Now you just hold off that man!"

In the sudden silence she stomped over to stand directly between Nathan Reynolds and his two victims. "Who do you think you are, laying into Will Green like that?"

Nathan Reynolds had no choice but to take a single step away from the woman. "But he said—"

"I know what he's saying, and I know what he's doing. He's working hard for a man who's never learned the value of a simple *thank you kindly*!"

Will called over, "That's all right, Miss Connie. I don't mind."

"Well, you should, Will Green. You most certainly should!"

Clearly the doctor was not used to being addressed in such a fashion. "I . . . He . . . You . . ."

"Hmph. That's the best you can do with all your citified ways?" She squinted at the doctor. "Now if I recollect correctly, you are *supposed* to be *doctoring*. Which I suggest you do with a lot less *yelling* around here for *all* our sakes."

Nathan Reynolds stared at her in utter confusion. "You're the mayor's assistant."

"Assistant mayor, if you please!" A movement caught her attention, and she wheeled about to glare at the people clustered in the clinic doorway, watching the fireworks. "What do you folks think you're watching, a show?" When that did not have them moving fast enough, she finished with, "If you're sick you shouldn't be standing, and if you ain't you shouldn't be here!"

Their retreat was made in total silence. But the doctor was made of sterner stuff. "I remember now." He gave one of his sharp little nods. "You're the one who ruined that thirty-four Terraplane pickup."

That focused Connie's rage back on the doctor. She waved a furious hand in an arc that started an inch in front of his nose and stopped so it was pointing back at Hattie. "You listen up real good, now. The next time you address this angel of a receptionist, I'd *strongly* advise you to begin with a simple *how-do*!"

The doctor looked from one woman to the other, clearly baffled. "How-do?"

"Well, that's a start. A small one, but a start." She snorted her derision. "And that truck happens to be a nineteen thirty-six, for your information."

The eyes began to narrow. "I told you they—"

Connie took a single menacing step toward him. "I came here full of friendliness and light. But if you don't stop with your nonsense right here and right now, we're gonna see the sparks fly!"

When Nathan Reynolds clenched his jaw shut, she gave a nod. "That's better. Now then. We'll all just start over here." She took as much of a breath as her anger allowed. "My uncle is a man of some renown in these parts. And he's the *second* most ornery man I've ever met in all my born days. Poppa Joe has got it into his head that you need to come up and meet him, don't ask me why. I'd just as soon hand him a live copperhead. But Poppa Joe don't bend easy and he lets go of ideas even harder. And I am fed up to my back teeth coming over here and giving you further chances to act nasty!"

She planted fists on her hips. "So this is what's gonna happen, sir. Tomorrow morning I'm picking you up and I'm taking you to Wilkes Mountain."

Nathan was absolutely astonished by the pronouncement. "Come again?"

"You need your ears cleaned out? I said . . ." Connie was halted by a gentle hand on her arm.

Hattie came up beside them, smiled Connie to silence, and spoke to Nathan in her quiet soothing way. "Poppa Joe Wilkes is famous in these parts. He guards his privacy too. An invitation to go see the old man is a genuine honor."

"Amen to that," Will Green called over. "I ain't been up Wilkes Mountain more'n two, three times my whole life. Give anything to go see the old man again. He's something, Poppa Joe is."

"You really should go meet Poppa Joe," Hattie said, giving her soft smile to both combatants.

Connie found her anger fading, her shoulders slumping in tired resignation. "I'm sorry I got cross," she muttered to the ground at her feet. "But Poppa Joe has been after me for weeks. I'd be grateful if you'd come."

There was a moment of silence before Nathan Reynolds snapped out in his customary harsh voice, "Make it midafternoon. I've got some things to see to in the morning." He turned on his heel and started for the clinic, shouting at Will as he walked. "And you get back to work!"

When the clinic door had slammed closed, Connie sighed and said, "Somebody's gonna shoot that man. And I hope they do it real slow."

"I suppose I've heard a less pleasing invitation than the one you just gave Doc Reynolds," Hattie said quietly. "But right now I can't seem to remember when."

Now that it was over, Connie felt very tired. "Every time I've met that man, I declare he's gotten me so riled I could grind riverbottom rock with my bare teeth."

Will Green called over, "I ain't sure you oughtta gone and said what you did back there, Miss Connie."

"Being the town's only doctor doesn't give him the right to make hearth rugs out of the rest of us, Will."

"But Miss Connie—"

Hattie said, "Not now, Will. Please." She grasped Connie's arm and pulled her across the street. "We need to talk."

Connie walked alongside her friend and said, "I can't for the life of me understand what's keeping you here with this man."

"Because I don't want him to go out and hire some sweet

young thing who lets him stomp all over her and crush her spirit, that's why."

"Now tell me the real reason."

Hattie guided them over to the riverbank before quietly replying, "I've had the strongest feeling that God wants me here."

Connie stared at the woman with strong-boned features and quiet country ways. "Girl, have you gone all soft in your mind?"

"I knew you wouldn't understand, that's why I didn't tell you before. But that's how it's felt. Ever since the moment I heard Ida May had quit, I felt like the Lord was asking me to come help out."

The power of Hattie's quiet words left her shaken. Connie found herself recalling weeks back, on the first drive into town after Dawn's return. Just as when the young girl had said she had prayed for Connie, she sensed a silent challenge.

When Connie did not respond, Hattie went on. "You shouldn't let him get you so riled."

"Yeah, well, I've got myself a couple of other pots simmering on the stove today." Connie let her other worries show. "There's a big money fight brewing over Richmond way. Looks like I'm going to have to spend my Sunday trying to find people at home and twisting their arms while their guards are down."

"It's a shame, you having to work on a Sabbath."

"If I don't, the battle will be lost before the meeting starts Monday morning." Connie stared down at the water for a time, wondering why giving into anger always left her feeling lonely afterward. "I missed Dawn this morning. Stopped by the house to pick her up, but there wasn't anybody around."

"That was my fault. It didn't hit me until we were into town that neither of us thought to give you a call." It was Hattie's turn to sigh and shake her head. "I drove her so we could get in some more quality arguing."

Connie looked at her oldest friend. Hattie's smile lines were pinched into crow's-feet, the eyes dark with worry. "What's the matter with Dawn?"

"You need to talk with that girl. She's got it in her head to marry Duke Langdon."

Once more Connie felt the world lurch beneath her feet. "Oh, Hattie, no. Tell me it's not true."

"I wish I could." Hattie wound her fingers through the colored beads around her neck. "I should never have let her start seeing that man in the first place."

"But Dawn is just a baby."

Hattie turned toward her, the motion like that of a nervous bird. "Honey, you been looking through the wrong end of your glasses."

"I don't wear spectacles and never have."

"You know exactly what I am talking about. Dawn is twenty. She'll be twenty-one in less than two months. Twenty is how old I was when I married Chad."

For some reason, the mention of his name brought out all the old aches and pains, like an illness that had not fully healed. Not even after two decades. "But that was then."

"Yeah, well, that argument don't carry as much weight as it should around our house."

"What does Chad say?"

"That he loves his daughter, and he hopes she knows her own heart and mind." Hattie sighed and shook her head. "I never thought the day would come when I'd be wishing my man wasn't so all-fired agreeable."

Her man. Strange how the words seemed to rock Connie so this day. Hattie's man. Hattie's daughter. And now Connie was to lose what little connection she had to the lovely girl she wished with all her heart was her own. Lose her to a man she detested.

Duke Langdon was a picture-perfect mountain man, tall and slender with sky-blue eyes that seemed most comfortable searching the nearest horizon. He had been the local football star, quarterbacking the tiny high school to the state play-offs three years running. He had then played in Charlottesville for a year, captaining the university freshman squad and playing the occasional endgame with the varsity team. Then, without reason or discussion, Duke Langdon had come home.

Some people said it was because the slow-talking man simply could not cut the mustard with the school's tough scholastic requirements. Others said it was because he didn't really have what it took to play big-league ball. Still others said the man preferred the easy mountain life, working in his daddy's store and spending his weekends fishing and hunting the local hills. Whatever the reason, one thing most people agreed on was that Duke Langdon was a nice fellow. Simple and a little slow and probably too well off and too handsome for his own good. But nice.

Connie said, "That man can't be playing with a full deck."

"Oh, I don't know." Hattie sounded resigned. "He's probably got all his cards. He just deals them out a little slow."

"Not to mention the fact that he's a cradle robber. How old is he? Twenty-eight?"

"Twenty-nine. And that dog won't hunt either. You're forgetting Chad is six years older than I am."

"Hattie, you're just gonna have to stop stomping on all my best arguments."

She turned desperate eyes toward Connie. "What on earth are we gonna do?"

"If it didn't work talking to Dawn, maybe somebody should try shaming Duke to his senses." Connie started back toward her car. "I'll talk to him when I get back from Richmond. And don't you worry. I'm sure we can bring Dawn around to our way of thinking."

Eight

Nathan Reynolds carried his second cup of coffee out on the front porch and sat listening to the same sound that had lulled him to sleep the night before. Here it was the last week in November, and the night's frost melted swiftly with the dawn. The river's quiet whispers had lulled him to sleep, and been there to wake him up as well. And like almost all of his mornings in this strange little town, his awakening had been free of the haunting cries that had so scarred his past two years.

He had never needed much rest. Living on five hours of sleep was a knack most medical students forced themselves to acquire, but for Nathan it had been as natural as breathing. Since his attack, however, he had slept even less. Two hours some nights, four others, and these came only after long and sweaty battles. But here in Hillsboro he found himself sleeping six, seven, even eight hours on occasion. And he was waking up more easily than he had in two long years.

After his collapse, waking had become as awful as sleeping. He fought against rising from slumber as hard as he did against sleeping in the first place. He went to bed dreading not just the nightmares. Those had been with him since the early days of his residency. No. He feared most the cries that continued long after sleep left, like ghosts who gained entry into his mind and heart while he was defenseless.

They had hung on longer and longer, those ghosts, until they took over his waking hours as well. An attack, the doctors had called it. Truer words had never been uttered. He hated the way his mornings had become battlegrounds, waking to the cries of unseen foes, feeling helpless to do anything but rage against the world.

But not now, not here. Nathan sipped his coffee and sat through the early chill. Dawn came slow to this valley. The fan of light streaming off the eastern peaks grew in strength, slowly dispelling the shadows down below. Birds flitted about the feeder at the house next door. Nathan was separated from his neighbors by a border of roses and magnolias, and more lawn than he had seen in years.

There was a road between him and the river, but it belonged mostly to the local kids and their bikes. Any cars that dared enter this lane threaded their way carefully around strollers and kickball games and jump ropes.

After his lonely dinners, he had taken to standing there on the porch and listening to the chatter and the laughter and the kids singing their little chanted songs. He was eating very well here, especially since Thanksgiving. When he had made it clear he was not interested in accepting invitations, people brought the celebration to him. His refrigerator and kitchen table remained filled to overflowing with casserole dishes and salad bowls and pie plates, all compliments of townsfolk who rushed in and shook his hand and wished him well and left, their movements slow and quick at the same time.

Nothing in his eleven years of medicine had prepared him for such a welcome. He caught sight of desperation in some of the faces. He felt it in the way they had grasped his hand and not wanted to let go. He heard it in the unspoken pleas, and the way they apologized for the state of the clinic. Everybody who stopped by said something to that effect, what a shame it was that he had found it in such a terrible state. Terrible. But they hoped he would be happy here. All of them. Their quiet fervor made it seem as though they took his happiness as a personal concern.

He set down his empty cup, and wondered if there had ever been a patient back in the city who had wondered about his being happy.

Nathan Reynolds stayed where he was and watched the sun clear the hills and warm the valley. Such quiet inactivity did not come naturally. There had been days back in the dark times when medication had kept him immobile. But not from desire. Not until now. He did not understand what kept him sitting there, watching the other houses come alive and the children fill the street before his house. But the world moved more slowly here. There were new mysteries confronting him, things he could only understand through such quiet moments of reflective inspection.

It was almost noon before he went back inside. The house itself was another amazement, two-story and brick with granite corners and stone borders around tall sash windows. Even the pillared porch was floored in rough-hewn granite. The old doctor had left it to the town, with instructions to give it to whoever took his place. His first few nights Nathan had walked through the old place, taking in the sixteen-foot-high ceilings, the crown moldings, the lead-paned windows, the sprung oak floors, the light fixtures which most likely had originally been fired by gas. The locals had even polished the kitchen floor for him, and put in a stove and refrigerator so new the tags were still in place. Still now, six weeks since his arrival, the house smelled of beeswax and fresh paint.

Shadows made dusty by the doctor's old furniture were there to greet him as he entered. He stopped in the doorway to the living room and pushed the light button. He had never seen anything like these light switches, one button for on and another for off. He pressed the on button and blinked as the room's two chandeliers and six wall fixtures and four corner lamps all flashed on. Somebody had come through and polished all the little crystal baubles and changed all the bulbs. The effect was like a perpetual camera flash.

After a solitary lunch he went back into the living room and picked up the house's only telephone. It was round and black Bakelite and had a circular dial set in the front. The cord was covered by black woven cloth. He gave the long-distance operator a number from memory.

When the familiar voice answered, Nathan said, "Hope I'm not disturbing your Saturday routine."

"Are you kidding? I've been growing worried, Nathan. You should have called me weeks ago." Margaret Simmons was both senior hospital administrator and dear friend. One of the few who had stood by him through the dark days. "How are you settling in?"

"Time warp doesn't even begin to describe this place."

"Oh, come on. It can't be that bad."

"I'm holding a phone that could have been a prop in a Ronald Coleman movie." He swung in a slow circle, the telephone cord wrapping itself around his feet. "Their clinic is equipped with stuff that went out with top hats and horse-drawn carriages."

Margaret was in her early sixties, at the top of her field, and had the ability to make every one of her four hundred staff members feel a vital part of the team. "They need you, then."

"I saw a baby right after I got here. Typical pyloric stenosis. The parents were driving forty miles over country roads to a doctor who had never heard of Maalox."

"I'll have to take your word for all of that." A pause, then, "How are you, Nathan?"

"Too early to tell." He took a breath. "I've been sleeping pretty well, though."

"That's something."

"And I wake up feeling okay."

"Even better." Another hesitation. "I take it you're not interested in things around here."

Even the sudden yearning was not enough to draw him back. The wounds were still too raw. "Not yet. I'm still busy handling this one day at a time."

"Good boy." A muffled voice in the background, then, "Hubby Matt says to give you his best."

"Thanks. Listen, you think any of that hospital equipment you pass on to the medical schools could be rerouted to me?"

"Things are really that bad?"

"Margaret, I've got to crank-start the autoclave."

"A joke. Good. That's very good. What do you need?"

"A complete theater for minor ops, emergency room gear, lighting, cabinets, cardiograph monitor, the works." He ran a hand through his hair. "If I had a real emergency I'd be better off using a gun."

"Okay, tell you what." Margaret stopped and thought awhile. "Anything to do with our equipment has to go through proper channels. Even the castoffs. It'll take me, oh, maybe three months to get the paperwork in order and have the board okay—"

"Three months, Margaret, come on, I was hoping for something like three days."

"Nathan, I can't just toss our stuff in the back of a station wagon and send it off, not even for you. But if you think you'll hold out that long, I'll go to the trouble. For you."

He found the commitment fiercely threatening, but even so found himself replying, "I'll try."

"Good man. From the sounds of things, they need you. And I'll get off a few boxes of emergency supplies to you as soon as I possibly can. Things I can sweep under the administrative rug."

"Thanks, Margaret. You're a pal."

"You take care of yourself down there. Stay away from pythons and piranhas."

"I think you've got the wrong continent, but I get the message."

Nathan hung up the phone, energized by the tiny connection to the outside world.

Then he recognized the woman getting out of the car in his drive, and the energy seeped away with his exasperated sigh. He went to grab a coat.

Nine

The road leading out of Hillsboro rose at a deceptive angle. It was only when the trees opened for a moment to reveal the rapidly descending valley floor that Nathan realized how high they were climbing. Connie handled the big car and the curves with practiced ease. The Oldsmobile was relatively new, yet it bore scars similar to those he had seen on her truck.

He had no idea what he was doing, going for a drive with this strange woman. But something drew him to her. Which was bizarre, given that they had absolutely nothing in common. Not to mention the fact that every time they had met, they had argued fiercely.

But it was not just Connie Wilkes who perplexed Nathan. All these hillfolk baffled him utterly. Nothing in his past had prepared him for such a place. It was as though time simply did not matter here. Nor the outside world.

And the way this woman had yelled at him the day before. Nathan had grown so accustomed to respect and subservience around the hospital that he felt as though someone had shaken him awake. He had stood there waiting for his own anger to rise up and confront her. But nothing had happened. He had felt stripped bare.

Nathan found himself glancing over to her from time to time, observing her as she drove. Her face held to angular lines and far too much strength ever to be called beautiful. More like handsome in a countrified way. The little makeup she wore had been applied with impatient haste. Her hair was mostly darkish blond, but there were streaks of a deeper russet color, almost like the surrounding autumn-flecked trees.

Connie cleared her throat, displaying a touch of nerves in the formal way she said, "I have to thank you for coming out like this."

"I'm the one who should be grateful." He found himself adopting the same stiffness. "I haven't been past the city limits since I arrived."

"You have to watch that. A valley town like ours can begin to close in on you. Time in the hills or time in the city, everybody needs one or the other."

The road took a sharper curve, and for an instant the valley spread out below him. Harvest colors swept down the steep-sided slopes, as though great autumn hands cradled the little town. The river caught the afternoon light and waved at him. "It certainly is beautiful here."

"Yes." It was her turn to cast a nervous glance. "Have you made any decision about how long you'll be staying?"

"Right now I'm just taking it one day at a time." He wanted to say more, to try and explain how that was the rule for all his life. The desire to speak was the strangest part of a very strange day. But he held his tongue.

She accepted the news with a glum little nod. "We sure need you."

Nathan opened his mouth to continue, but his old fears instantly resurfaced. The banked-up apprehension that had colored so much of his life these past two years rose like a beast in the car there between them. And he responded with the only weapon he had left. His anger.

He groused, "The state's Department of Health does a lousy job of seeing to your needs. Either that or you people haven't taken the time to apply correctly for a replacement doctor."

Connie's mouth tightened into a thin line. "I've spent months pleading with every official I could get to hold still. County and state both."

He didn't like the acid tone he had brought out, but he didn't know what to do about it. And his own anger was still there, fighting back the whispering ghostly tendrils. "Maybe you didn't do it right."

A flush rose from the collar of her blouse. "It's my business to handle outside officialdom. I did *everything* right."

"I can well imagine," he muttered. "Considering how you handled yourself at the clinic yesterday, you probably raised the hackles of everybody involved. Now the town's had to pay."

"That's just not true," she cried angrily. "The simple fact is, there aren't enough doctors willing to go out and serve in small isolated postings like our town." She shot a bitter glance his way. "Doctors these days are a lot more interested in making big bucks than serving needy people."

"So you say," he grumbled. But he knew there was truth in her words. Every medical journal was filled with ads pleading for doctors to serve in backwater towns and regions.

"You just hang on," Connie snapped back, then gunned the motor and spun the wheel. The big car roared in response, as though it had been waiting for this all along.

Nathan flinched. He could not help it. A branch leaped out and slapped the windshield right in front of his face. There was a groaning creak as a tree brushed down Connie's side of the car. The automobile bucked like a horse as it passed over a rain-washed gully. And the track grew continually steeper.

The path was two rocky furrows, and still it rose higher. The angle increased until Nathan was pressed back hard into his seat, and he seemed pointed straight toward the sky.

Connie kept the accelerator down hard and handled the wheel with steady ease. The trees continued to slap and scratch at the car. The tires slipped and grabbed and bucked and bounced. They rose ever higher.

Suddenly they popped up above the first line of trees, and he risked a glance behind him. The world was stretched out in all its glory, the valley lost beneath a soft afternoon haze.

In a flash his anger was gone. Which was very strange, because rarely did it ever release him so easily. Nathan had come to expect that once he found the day's rage, it remained a part of him until nightfall. Yet here he was, racing up a steep hill, his anger spent. He felt so free he had to speak, to share the unexpected freedom. He turned back in time to meet the next rise, and said, "I'd hate to think what this is like in snow."

"Don't try it without four-wheel drive." Her clipped tone still carried the ire he had ignited. "Come to think of it, don't try it alone at all for a while."

"Where are we headed?"

"I told you yesterday. Poppa Joe's. Almost there."

They crested a second ledge with a bouncing roar that popped the front tires into the air. Then they were down and racing through a broad meadow, one turned golden by the light and the season.

Nathan found himself caught by a desire to laugh out loud. He could not explain why. There was absolutely no reason for the sensation. Yet there he was, watching the high grass blur to either side, seeing a bevy of doves take flight in startled fear at their passage, feeling as though he had left the earth and all his cares behind, and for one brief instant was again a person who could laugh with the simple joy of living.

Too soon Connie pulled up in front of a ramshackle log cabin. The feeling passed as she cut the motor and muttered, "What on earth is *he* doing here?"

In the place of momentary joy rose a more familiar sadness. A wishing he could recapture whatever it was that had been there in that brief sweet instant. He followed her angry glare and saw a brand new Chevy pickup parked to one side of the cabin. "Who is it?"

"Never mind." Her tone was terse, her movements very controlled as she opened her door and climbed from the car. "Come on."

She walked over to where an old man was looking down at a metal washtub, his hands on his knees. A young boy knelt by his feet, and a tall handsome man stood alongside. They all were laughing. Only Connie's face was tight. As Nathan followed her toward the group, he knew an instant's regret for having provoked such a mood on such a pretty day.

The younger man noticed their approach, looked up, and stiffened in wary surprise. He was tall and lanky in a manner Nathan had come to recognize during his time up here, muscles like steel strapped to a frame etched from the hills themselves.

He wiped nervous hands down his trouser legs. "Well, hi there, Miss Connie. Poppa Joe said I could come by and—"

"I'll get to you in a minute, Duke Langdon." She stopped by the washtub, gave the contents one glance, then said to the old man, "I brought him like you said. Now you can settle something once and for all. When did you buy your Hudson pickup?"

The old man seemed to unwind as he rose to full height. He was taller even than the young man, a rickety giant of a man.

Nathan could not help but stare. The old man had a face carved of the same granite as the mountains. His chin pushed out to where it appeared ready to touch the hawk-billed nose. Silver hair as thick as a lion's mane swept back from a broad flat forehead. But what planted Nathan firmly where he stood were the man's eyes.

Nathan's first impression was of a painting come to life. The old man had the deep-hard gaze of pictures he had seen as a boy, pictures hanging on the walls of the Smithsonian in Washington. The paintings had sent shivers down his spine and seemed to bring all the history books alive. The faces were of Revolutionary War heroes, whose gazes had pierced with impossible determination. Their eyes had reached out to strike him where he stood, searching across the centuries and demanding of him to be more than what he found comfortable. They had always seemed to ask of the younger Nathan, *Are you worthy? Have you earned what we fought and died for?*

The old man glanced his way only briefly, but it was enough to penetrate with that same severe passion. Poppa

Joe said, "This is how you was brought up to introduce folks, daughter?"

"Nathan Reynolds, Joseph Wilkes. Everybody alive calls him Poppa Joe. And this is Duke Langdon. The boy I don't know." She waved it all aside with an impatient gesture. "Now tell me when you bought your truck, Poppa Joe."

"The boy's name is Henry, Hank for short," Duke offered. His voice carried traces of the same tone and manner as Poppa Joe's. As did his face—all overlaid with the softness of an easier life. "He's the child of some good friends of mine. Say hello to Miss Connie and the doc, Hank."

The boy mumbled something, not looking up from the washtub.

Poppa Joe Wilkes looked blown from the cannon of untrammeled adventure. There was not an ounce of fat on his frame, nor a single soft line to his face. And his eyes. "I bought that there Hudson Terraplane in nineteen and thirty-six. And it sounds to me like you two have done climbed my mountain with a quarrel."

"There. Nineteen thirty-six. Just like I said." But there was no triumph to her tone. Connie crossed her arms and took a step back. "The smarmy doctor's done finally got something wrong."

"Daughter, I don't hold with talk like that, especially with first-time visitors. You oughtta know that by now." Poppa Joe walked over and extended his hand. "Welcome, Mr. Nathan. It's an honor making your acquaintance, sir."

"Likewise." Nathan accepted a handshake as hard as leather-covered stone. He hesitated, finding himself suddenly bashful. "I don't mean any disrespect, sir, but that truck of yours was made in thirty-four."

Connie snorted and kicked at a pebble.

"Now that may well be. I done bought it as a Christmas present for my Mavis, God rest her gentle soul. Picked it up the middle of January. Them was hard times, and folks didn't hold with change and fashion like they do now. It could've been a leftover." The old man looked skyward, his eyes holding a power to peel the heavens apart. "Heavy snows that winter. Had a dickens of a time getting it up my hill."

Connie stared at him, a look of utter consternation on her face. "You never told me that."

"Guess it didn't seem so all-fired important before. Don't seem so all-fired important now, neither." He had a way of speaking which was both gentle and commanding, as though he had long been comfortable with times of quiet. "Come on over here, Mr. Nathan. Got something you might like to see."

Nathan allowed himself to be guided over to the washtub. He shook hands with Duke. Then he looked down at the washtub, and said, "What on earth."

"Had a buddy whose dog whelped not long back." Duke's voice was quiet and slow. In time with the place and the old man. "Good hunting hound."

"The best," agreed the little boy, kneeling back down. "And Uncle Duke is buying me one of the puppies for my birthday. I'm gonna make him the best hunting dog what ever lived. You just wait and watch how I do with him."

"Well now, we'll just have to see about that, won't we." The old man eased himself down in slow, gradual stages. A long-fingered hand reached for the rim of the washtub and lifted it. Out tumbled seven whining, squeaking little puppies, all black and white and brown. They fumbled about on their oversized paws, shivering and sniffing the strange scent-laden air. "Sure do got the look of good hounds, don't they."

"Pick me out a winner, Poppa Joe," the boy said.

Duke explained to Nathan, "Never did meet a man who could spot a prize hunting dog like Poppa Joe."

"A winner ain't just in the picking, boy," the old man said. "You got to put in lotsa hard hours training him."

"I will, Poppa Joe." Hank's voice was solemn as his eyes. "I promise."

"All right, let's see now." He moved the puppies about like he was stirring a pot, pushing them, watching them move, stroking a gentle finger down their backs.

One of the puppies began following the finger as it moved, batting it with one timid paw. Poppa Joe picked him up, cradled him for a minute. "Need to let the fellow know your scent. No dog is raised up good with lessons alone. You got to give him love, and lots of it. Like little boys in that way, ain't they."

"I'll give him love every day, I promise, Poppa Joe."

"Fine, son. That's just fine." He stroked the puppy's muzzle, then set it down. Again the dog tried to hunt the hand, giving a high-pitched bark when it moved. "Feisty little fellow. Now let's see if he knows how to mind."

Poppa Joe stiffened his fingers and moved with lightning speed, popping a hand down on the hind quarters. The little dog squeaked its protest, but sat down. Poppa Joe moved his hand out in front of the dog's eyes, keeping it there. Nathan observed the heavy tremor which the old man could not control. The puppy sat where he was, head cocked to one side, and gave a tiny whine.

Poppa Joe rose slowly. "That there looks like a good'un to me."

Hank scooped up the puppy and held it close to his chest. "I'm gonna call him Duke. Like my uncle, 'cause he's my very best friend and he's promised to teach me hunting."

The tall young man said gently, "What do you say, now?"

"Thank you, Poppa Joe. Thank you, Uncle Duke. This is the bestest present I've ever got in my whole life."

"That's good, son. That's good. Now pick up those other puppies and put them back in the tub." Poppa Joe straightened with the stiff motions of the very old. He dusted off his trousers and said to Duke, "You got a good hand with the young'uns, son. When're you getting around to starting a family of your own?"

Nathan watched Duke cast a nervous glance over to where Connie was kicking another pebble. "Been thinking about that very thing."

Poppa Joe gave a single nod of approval. He then turned to Nathan and said, "I ain't heard talk of any family, Mr. Nathan."

"I'm not married, sir." It seemed incorrect to call such a stately man Poppa anything. "Never had the time."

"Ought to make yourself time for that." The strange mix of gentle strength robbed the words of any sting. "World can be a hard and lonely place without family."

Connie spoke up for the first time since receiving news of the truck. "This from a man who's been alone more years than I'd care to count."

"God granted me the perfect wife," the old man replied, clearly untouched by his niece's ire. "He gave us nigh on forty perfect years together. I don't know why He chose to take her from me, but He did. Mavis in memory is a finer thing than ever a second wife could be in body."

Hank used his free hand to pluck at Duke's sleeve. "Would you ask him, Uncle Duke?"

"You got yourself a voice, boy. Ask him yourself."

He cast Poppa Joe a shy look. "But he might say no."

"Never know until you try. Go ahead, now."

The boy swallowed. Nathan found himself staring at something he had not seen in years—a child struck by hero worship. "Poppa Joe," the boy stammered.

"Yes, son."

"Sir, will—will you show me your shootin'?"

The old man was about to say no. Nathan could see it in

his face. But then he looked not at the boy, but at Nathan himself. A single piercing glance, before he said, "Don't see why not."

The boy gave a little jump of delight, causing the puppy in his arms to squeal in alarm.

"Careful, now. Hand your dog to Duke. Connie, honey, think maybe you could find a soda pop bottle and my gun up in the house?"

She said nothing, just turned and walked up the steps. When she was inside, Poppa Joe asked more quietly, "Is her quarrel with the doctor or with you, Duke?"

"Me," Nathan said. "I'm sorry that—"

"No sir, Doc, you got that one wrong." Duke inspected his hunting boots. "I was gonna ask you about that too, Poppa Joe, but what with her showing up like this . . ."

He let his voice trail off as Connie reappeared carrying a glass bottle, a long-barreled rifle, and a box of shells. She handed them to her uncle, shot Duke a fiery look, and strode back a ways. Duke offered the ground at his feet a weary sigh.

Poppa Joe looked from one to the other, then turned to the boy and said, "Son, run this here bottle out and set it on the corner post back there by the woods."

The boy took the bottle, started away, then realized what he had just heard. He pointed and said, "That post out yonder, Poppa Joe?"

"Looks like a good one to me."

The boy turned and looked at his uncle. His eyes were

round moons. Duke said mildly, "Let me have the puppy. All right, run on, now."

"But, Uncle Duke, that's—"

"Go and do what Poppa Joe said."

"Yessir." Hank scampered off.

Only when the boy was halfway across the broad meadow did Nathan understand. The boy ran down the length of a ramshackle split-rail fence, headed for the *last* post. It was so far away that by the time Hank got there, all Nathan could see was the dark head bounding through the tall grass. Carefully the boy reached up and steadied the bottle, then turned and waved and sped back. Poppa Joe did not look in the boy's direction. Not once.

His eyes on the sky and the sunlit horizon, Poppa Joe said, "Mr. Nathan, think maybe you might like to stay up here with me a night? Evenings can be right pleasant up here in the hills."

Nathan already had the polite decline formed and in his mouth. Then he caught sight of Duke's expression. The young man was looking at him with something akin to awe.

Once more he felt caught up in things he had no understanding of. Yet there was something else now, a whisper as gentle as the afternoon breeze, a sense of being offered something priceless. Nathan found himself thinking of the old man's gaze, and almost in spite of himself, he said, "I'd be honored."

"That's good. That's real good. Duke, why don't you

bring yourself back up tomorrow morning, give the doc here a ride back down to town."

"Sure, Poppa Joe. Glad to do it."

He pitched his voice slightly higher. "You hear that, daughter?"

"I'm hearing. But I'm sure not understanding." Connie put her hands back on her hips. "Why on earth would you have a stranger up here, when you won't even see friends you've known all your life?"

"Just offering the doc here a little homespun hospitality. Ain't nothing the matter with that."

Connie shook her head, allowing her shoulders to droop. Nathan found himself sensing her confusion and defeat, which was very strange, for he had not felt anything except his own distress for a lifetime and more. Yet he did, and found a rightness there as well. What else could possibly be his first shared feeling other than the same confusion and defeat which had so scarred his own past few years.

Nathan found himself wishing there were some way to cross the gap between them, to step over to her and say something of comfort. But the act was beyond him. The moment and the sense of sharing was just too new. So he stood and watched as Connie walked to the car and opened her door.

Connie halted with one foot on the doorsill and called back over, "I've got to go to Richmond tonight. Something's come up."

"You have yourself a good trip, daughter." Poppa Joe rammed back the bolt-action lever. Then he had trouble picking a bullet from the box and fitting it into the barrel. His hands shook so that Nathan could hear the bullet rattle and scratch across the metal. "Don't work yourself too hard, mind."

Connie did not respond. She just stood there, leaning against the door. Watching.

Poppa Joe waited until the boy had returned and caught his breath. "All right, son. Now tell me what kinda wind we got ourselves here."

"Yessir, Poppa Joe." Hank dropped to his knees. His brow furrowed with concentration, he lifted a bit of earth and crumbled it, watching carefully as it drifted down. "Ain't hardly any at all, Poppa Joe. Just a little from the north."

"Yep, ain't much now. But you watch. Gonna be a blow tonight, and tomorrow we're gonna wake up to winter. North wind, he always starts quiet like. Moves like a big old hawk, riding the currents, silent and crafty and carrying death in his claws."

Nathan squinted and looked back at the bottle. It seemed impossibly far away, a tiny shard glimmering jewel-like on the distant post. He glanced back at the old man. As far as Nathan could tell, the old man had not glanced once at the distant post.

"You want to hunt these hills, son, you got to learn more than just how to track." Poppa Joe took a step towards the awe-struck boy, his walk as palsied as his hands. "You got to learn the mountain's ways. You got to have respect for God's creation, and learn the lessons He done wrote in the earth. You hear what I'm saying?"

"Yessir, Poppa Joe, I'm a'hearing."

The sense of timelessness Nathan had been feeling ever since his arrival gathered and grew in force, focusing down upon the moment. Nathan felt caught in an amber of immortal power. He was able to sense everything, capture it in sensations he knew would take ages to digest.

"God is all around us. He walks these hills Himself, and you can walk with Him, if you only learn the way. You got to be quiet, not with your mouth, but quiet with your *mind*. You got to be reverent in these hills, 'cause they're God's home. He gave them to us for a time, but make no mistake, they're His and His alone."

Everything seemed full of silent import. The way the tips of the grass breathed in unison, the slight chill spicing the afternoon sunlight, the way the young man and the boy hung on every word Poppa Joe spoke.

Poppa Joe looked down at the gun in his trembling hands. "We hunt and we eat what we take from God's bounty. But it ain't the hunting that's important. It's what we bring with us when we come, and take back with us when we leave. You remember that. God calls us to give our lives *meaning*. We do that by living with respect and love, for creation and for our neighbor. And whenever you're blessed with time up here, you treat these hills like you would a church. 'Cause God lives here. Make no mistake about that."

Then it happened. One moment the hands were shaking and holding the gun down at his waist, almost in offering. The next moment and the shot had already rung out in the still air. Nathan had not even seen the rifle move.

He felt himself jump with the shock of how swift it had happened. Glass shattered in the distance like faint chimes.

The mountains applauded the feat, great booming echoes back and forth from hillside to hillside for an impossibly long time.

Poppa Joe lowered the rifle, opened the bolt, blew out the plume of smoke from the barrel.

"*Doggone!*" The boy cried and jumped and pulled at Duke's sleeve. "Did you *see* that, Uncle Duke? Did you *see* that?"

Poppa Joe waited until the boy's shining eyes had returned to his ancient features, then he said, "You remember what I told you, son. These hills is God's home. You be sure and give His gift a worthy meaning in your young life."

Ten

By the time Connie came down the mountain, the Saturday afternoon was gradually giving way to a golden-hued evening. Connie spent the entire drive to Hattie's house mentally haranguing the doctor. And her uncle. Which even she had to admit was a little bizarre, since there were far more pressing problems awaiting her in Richmond. Not to mention the reason she was going by the Campbells' house this particular evening.

But her mind remained fixed on those men and their clannish gathering. She had felt utterly isolated, just some outsider good only to step and fetch.

What was far worse was how she had lost yet another argument with Nathan Reynolds. Connie gave an irritated shake to her head, forcing her hair back behind her shoulders. Well, it was the last time he'd ever have a chance to get the better of her. She would never go back to that clinic. Not even if she were bleeding from a dozen holes, she would not see him again. Nossir. Not even if her life depended on it.

She came over the rise and pulled into the Campbells'

drive and turned off the engine. And she sat there. Because she realized then she had no idea what on earth she was going to say.

Like a lot of the older hillside homes, the Campbells had added on to what once had been a log-and-slat cabin. Theirs had been done with taste and concern, each subsequent generation adding modern features and a bit more room. The original cabin was now the living room, a jutting front section whose forward-facing wall now held a grand plate-glass window. The walk leading from the drive to the front door was paved with the same Hillsboro stone that supported the two brick arms stretching out from the cabin.

More stone formed the corner joists and chimney. The result was a house of character, one that drew stares and slowed cars. Connie had often stared herself, especially on evenings when the front curtains were flung back and she could see figures moving about inside. And she would wonder how it might have been, had she argued less and listened more, both to Chad Campbell and to her own heart.

Back when Connie was young, she had thought the whole world waited and beckoned from just beyond the reach of the next valley. After her parents had died in a pile-up with a logging truck, her love of Chad Campbell had been just about the only thing that had tied Connie to the town.

They had dated all through Connie's final two years of high school, and the closer she came to graduation, the more Chad had mentioned marriage. Connie had fought against it tooth and nail, frightened for reasons she only half understood. But the worst of their fights had not been about getting married. The truly cataclysmic battles had been over Chad Campbell's dream.

Since childhood Chad had dreamed of opening a grocery store in the heart of Hillsboro. Back when Chad was young, his family had suffered every winter after snows had closed the road and Hillsboro's only grocery had raised its prices. Even though Connie had known the reasons and agreed with them in principle, she still did not see how an intelligent man like Chad Campbell could hold to selling vegetables to cranky hillfolk as the dream of a lifetime.

They had spent at least part of every evening arguing over the future. Connie had been born with a restless spirit, turned raw and chafing by the events of her teenage years. Chad's quietly stubborn mountain ways had driven her straight up the wall.

Perhaps even then she had known that to have taken the man from his home would have killed him, for Chad's roots ran deep in the valley's hardscrabble soil. Perhaps if she had truly loved him enough she would have heard all the messages this quiet man had never put into words. It was one of those questions which continued to attack her in the weak moments of many sleepless nights.

LIVERY
STABLE
Campbell's
Grocery
SALE

She had finally made it out of Hillsboro, winning a scholarship to study business administration at the prestigious regional college, William and Mary. But the longer she had been away, the more Connie had pined for the hills and the tiny valley town which before had left her feeling as though she could not breathe.

But just as she was working up the nerve to write Chad and tell him he had been right all along, she had received a wedding invitation. Chad had decided to marry Hattie, Connie's oldest friend.

Hattie had always admired Connie and her spirit, yet had also realized that the valley was to be the place where she lived and died. Hillsboro remained the only home she ever wanted, needed, yearned for. Connie had attended the wedding and listened to all the folks say they had never seen such a perfect match. The words had scarred her heart like a branding iron.

The day after his marriage to Hattie, Chad had taken every cent he could save, beg, or borrow and bought the old livery stable at the far end of Main Street. Over the double glass doors, up above where the striped awning kept the summer sun off the racks of fresh produce, the finely etched wording for Smith's Livery and Horse Trading was still legible. That half-moon of wood was the only part of the entire place which had not been stripped down, repainted, polished, and spruced up until it was beyond all recognition.

A figure appeared in the Campbells' doorway, one whose golden hair formed a halo around her shadowy form. Dawn left the comfort of her house and started toward the car. Connie's heart ached at the sight of Dawn's hesitant step. Ever since she had been old enough to walk, Dawn's every hello for Connie had been enthusiastic, a sharing of the joy that welled up from within that bright-eyed little girl.

She was a child no longer. The young woman peered through the passenger door, studying Connie with an adult's gaze. Finally she opened the car door and slipped inside.

Dawn sat there a moment in silence, and then said, "You were taking so long, I decided to come on out and make it easier for you."

Connie swallowed down the sudden welling of longing for all that had been, and all that had never been granted a becoming. Her arguments were dust in the wind, scattered and gone. The only thing she could manage was a shaky, "Don't do this, honey. Please."

The Campbell home stood upon a knoll which had once been the high point of steeply sloping farmland. From her place behind the wheel, Connie could look out over both the house and the valley. Though the sun had descended behind the western ridges, streams of light turned the high reaches to shades of burnished bronze. The valley was lost to gathering shadows, while little star-flecks of light appeared to mark the way home.

When Dawn remained silent, Connie risked a glance over, and felt the breath catch around her heart. The girl's face was captured by the fading light of day, softened with timeless hues, filled with the wisdom of sadness. Her eyes remained steady on Connie, waiting for the older woman to face her full on.

Connie did so reluctantly. Everything about this new side to Dawn unsettled her. She could feel the child she had nurtured and loved slipping through her fingers like mercury, forcing her to confront a stranger. One who seemed to know more about Connie than she did herself.

Only when Connie had released her hold on the wheel and slid around on the seat did Dawn ask, "Why didn't you ever marry, Aunt Connie?"

There was another catch to the air, one that made it hard to answer. But the gathering night and the light in Dawn's eyes demanded honesty, even if it seared her insides to respond. "You know I once had a shine for your daddy."

"Sure. Then you went away to college. After that you got hired by the county and came back home."

"There was a boy then. It was the pastor's older brother."

"Reverend Blackstone?" Surprise lilted her tone. "I didn't know he had a brother."

"Julius Blackstone left town the year before you were born." All these secrets reappearing. Things she had thought buried and forgotten. "He wanted me to come with him. But by then I'd finished my visiting in the outside world. I had gone out, seen all I wanted to, and known I was meant to live out my days in Hillsboro."

"That's sad. But still it doesn't mean there couldn't have been somebody else."

"The problem with growing old in a small town is, everybody has a past."

"You're not old."

"People tend to see you in light of what you've done. All your mistakes are out in the open." Connie felt defeated by what she could not express. "I grew more involved in my work and let other things, like romance, fade away."

The moment seemed to swell with the past, until it was almost natural for Dawn to give voice to the unspoken. "You still wish it was Daddy, don't you?"

Connie wondered at how the dimming light seemed to be captured by Dawn's eyes. "How did you learn about me and Chad?"

"Oh, I think I've always known. I remember how you used to look at him, and how Momma watched you two when you were in a room together."

I never knew that, Connie started to say, but the words did not seem to want to come out. So she sat there, held by the soft truth and by all that had never been.

"When I was still real young I asked Momma about it once. She said God had given us Aunt Connie so that if anything ever happened to her, there would be someone to take care of me and Daddy."

I never knew that either, Connie wanted to respond, but her throat had swollen shut.

"I thought it was the most natural thing in the world to have two mothers. I always had two daddies, God the Father and Pop. So why not two mothers? I never did understand how other children made it through life with just one of each."

Dawn then did the most natural thing in the world, which was to slide over and give Connie a fierce hug. "I love you, Aunt Connie. I wish there was something I could do to give you the life you deserve."

Connie felt captured by the words. The little girl she had helped raise was no longer there. Instead she watched as a woman slid back to the other door, gave her a lingering glance, and said with studied calm, "Duke Langdon and I are getting married. It would mean more than I could ever say if you would give us your blessing."

Never, Connie wanted to say. She felt her fingernails dig into the seat cover with the strain of trying to fight out the word. But she could not speak. Something clenched at her throat.

Dawn watched her face with the same sad wisdom she had brought with her to the car. She opened the door and stood, then leaned back over and said, "I love you with all my heart, Aunt Connie."

She sat and watched this stranger who once had been her heart's delight walk away. She watched as Dawn entered the home which was not hers and never would be. And she felt a thousand years old.

The evening was impossibly loud.

Nathan sat on Poppa Joe's front porch and watched crickets and lightning bugs fight for space in the still air. The temperature was more suited to September, comfortable even this late into evening. Little fluttering shapes suggested there were bats about, but they kept their distance and flew so fast Nathan could not be sure. Then there came a rending screech, like a foot-long nail being pried out of steel. Nathan demanded, "What on earth was that?"

"Horned owl. Makes some kinda racket, don't it? You listen, now. The mate's around here somewhere." Just as the words were spoken came the equally loud response. "There you are. Them owls, they mate for life. They'll get apart a ways, and screech back and forth like that, trying to scare prey toward one or the other."

"You know these woods," Nathan observed. The words sounded lame, but were so full of truth they had to be spoken.

"Like the back of my hand." No boasting there. A simple agreement to all Nathan could not express. The chair squeaked with the sound of his turning. "Guess it's kinda like you and your doctoring."

"I know my field," Nathan agreed.

"They're folks up these parts, they figure if you don't know the hills, why, you don't know nothing. I'm eighty-two years old and I ain't never been farther afield than Charlottesville, and only been there once. But I know folks who speak thus are just plain wrong."

"It's easy to think the world ends at your doorstep," Nathan said, awash in memories.

"Son, you just spoke some kinda truth." Poppa Joe leaned forward, a shadow of movement as he spit over the rail. "Folks is always comforted by what they know, and scared by what they don't."

Nathan felt no need to press the conversation, which was unnatural. Silence had been a hated foe since the day. That was how he thought of it now—the day. It was easier than trying to recall all the time before and after. Gather all the horror of his nighttime ghosts rising to take over his daytime world, and package it into a single small unit, measurable and manageable. The day.

There were too many stars for just one night. Nathan leaned over far enough to see beyond the porch's edge. A silver river ran in eternal stillness overhead. Even without the moon, the light was enough to wash the meadow in ghostly white.

When the old man spoke again, it was as though the pause had only been for an instant, and not the better part of an hour. "Them same folks, now, they're the ones who go to the doctor for the birthing and the dying and never once in between. You ever met the like?"

"Not me. Where I'm from, if somebody gets the sniffles, they're calling for an appointment."

"Well, that right there'd be a problem, now, since most of them hill families don't have no phones. They're a dying breed, though. Less of 'em every year."

"Hard to believe there are still people out here without telephones."

"No phone, no electricity, no light except maybe a kerosene lamp. 'Less they got themselves a Coleman. You know what a Coleman is, son?"

"No idea whatsoever."

The old man hacked a laugh. "I like you, son. There ain't much foppery to your thinking or your talking. You strike me as a straight-walkin' man."

"Why, thank you, sir." Nathan was genuinely touched. "I take that as a compliment."

"Back when I was a boy, a Coleman was the cat's pajamas. Burned coal dust. You'd pump the gauge, build up a pressure, then light the lamp. First time I ever did read the Book after dark was the night my pappy brought home a coal-dust Coleman."

"Sounds like a bomb in the making."

"Aye now, it was that. Get a crack in the base, that thing'd go off like lightning. Lost a few families in the valley, we did. They took to sleeping with the light left on, thing got too heated up and took 'em straight to Glory."

A shadow drifted by, with wings impossibly long. "Owl. Big'un. Must be headed off for the other side. We're talking overloud for his liking." Poppa Joe paused, then picked up the thread of his earlier thought. "The ones who don't hold to doctoring, now, they carry on with a passel of home remedies. Good'uns, by and large. Stood the test of seeing a dozen generations and more through the trials and tribulations of this world. Nettle poultice, you ever used that one?"

Nathan had to laugh. "Can't say that I have."

"Good for young'uns what laying with the wet chest. Draws it out. You ever coated a body's throat with tincture of merthiolate?"

"I believe I've heard of that being used."

"Dead straight it's used. Best thing there is for the strep."

"This is like I'm sitting here listening to the last century come alive again."

"Ain't the last century, son. Ain't even last year. This is the here and now talking to you."

"And what happens when these home remedies don't work?"

"They die, son. They die. Lot of that going around these parts."

Nathan waited for the wheezy laugh, and when it didn't come, felt the weight of his own lost battles. "Lot of that everywhere."

"Them folks, you know what they call the doctor? The Gatekeeper. You ever heard tell of that before?"

"No." The night drew in around him. The night and a thousand hillside nights before. "No, I haven't."

"Yessir. Gatekeeper, he comes riding up on his big horse, with the specter in the black robe nigh on behind. That's the way it was in the high country, I reckon, for most of our people's time here. The village Gatekeeper, he might protect the young'un from the grim reaper for a little while yet, but not often, and more seldom still for very long."

Nathan felt as though the night had slammed the breath from his body. All the quiet mockery, all the silent derision he had felt for these country ways since his arrival, all was punched from his mind by the old man's words. In that instant, he felt closer to those strangers in the hills than anyone else on earth.

While he was still recovering, Poppa Joe rose to his feet, his joints seeming to creak with the floorboards. "Time we was getting a'bed, son. Dawn'll be rising us before you know it."

Nathan overslept, which was a very bad thing. The hour before dawn, when his guard was lowest, the nightmare came and captured him.

It was the same dream he had known ever since the breakdown, the image that had finally become a part of his waking world. Tiny arms reached up, tiny voices crying for help, and he was helpless to do anything at all. He stood trapped and unable to move, his feet embedded in concrete, struggling to act and reach and comfort and heal. And when it seemed that he might finally break free, the voices started going quiet. One by one they simply went away. The noise died, and with it the children died as well. His children. All of them turning to ghosts before his very eyes.

He awoke with a gasp so strong the intake raised him to a sitting position. Nathan sat there, trying to bring his heart rate down to a sustainable level. He heard the thump and creak of footsteps, and he raised his eyes. For the longest moment he could not remember where he was.

Then the door moaned its way open, and Poppa Joe Wilkes stood in the doorway, a steaming cup in one hand.

"You make more noise wakin' up than a bear at first thaw." He walked over and offered Nathan the cup. The hand shook so that the steaming liquid sloshed over the sides. "Figured I might as well come on in and say hidy."

He accepted the mug without meeting the old man's gaze. "I overslept."

"Don't matter none. World's still out there, dawn's moving slow as ever. Come on out when you're ready, I'll fix us some grub."

Nathan drank the coffee as he dressed. When he entered the main cabin, he found Poppa Joe busily stirring an iron skillet. "Coffee's in the pot there. I'm just fixing up a mess of grits and eggs. Thought mebbe we'd get ourselves an early start."

Nathan walked across the scarred plank floor. The ceiling was higher than he had expected, built to fit the man at the stove. The coffee pot was an ancient affair and smoke-blackened. "I'm not much on breakfast."

"Use that rag there to pour the coffee, save yourself some skin." He kept patting at the skillet's contents. "Need something solid in your gullet, son."

"My gullet." The towel was as black as the coffee pot. Nathan wrapped it around the handle and lifted the pot from its position at the corner of the wood-burning stove. The coffee poured out treacly-thick. "I'm not certain I could find that on an anatomy diagram."

"Now you're funnin' me. Sit yourself down over there." Poppa Joe ladled out eggs onto a metal plate, then added a spoonful of grits from an elderly pot. He set the plate down in front of Nathan, went back and made another for himself. He eased himself down into the chair.

Poppa Joe folded his long hands and brought his forehead down to meet them. The action was so fast and natural that Nathan almost missed the fact that Poppa Joe was about to pray.

"Lord in heaven, bless us and bless this day and bless this here food. We thank Thee, Lord, for all that is. Amen."

Poppa Joe raised his eyes in time to catch sight of Nathan's discomfort. He nodded once, picked up his fork, and pointed at Nathan's plate. "Get yourself into that lot there. Biscuits and bacon'll wait till we're back."

Nathan lifted his fork and patted the scrambled eggs. They were drier than hospital eggs that had rested in an overhot steamer through morning rounds. He felt Poppa Joe watching him, so he tried to scoop some up. They scattered across his plate like oddly shaped yellow marbles. "Back from where?"

"You'll see. Got something I want to show you."

Nathan knew he was being watched, and he did not want to disappoint his host. He plucked an edge from the glutinous lump of grits, and used that to glue some eggs to his fork. He chewed once and swallowed quickly. The mixture was pretty awful, but the coffee was bitter enough to mask the flavor. He ate with grim determination, chasing down each mouthful like medicine.

Poppa Joe eyed the empty plate with approval. "That's the spirit. Young feller like you's got to eat right."

Nathan pushed himself erect with both hands. His belly felt like he'd swallowed a bowling ball. "Where are we headed?"

"Here, put this on." Poppa Joe handed him a patched and ancient hunting jacket. When Nathan hesitated, he smiled and said, "Don't you worry none. Been washed since last year, and all the fleas that bit me done died an awful death."

"It's not that. I just don't know if I need something this heavy."

The grin broadened to reveal teeth too brilliant to be false. "You done forgot what I told you yesterday."

"What, oh yes, about the north wind. No, I didn't . . ." Nathan watched as the old man stumped to the door and flung it back. He stepped over, took one look, and gasped aloud.

Poppa Joe moved away. "Got you some wool socks and boots warming by the stove."

But Nathan could not move. Nothing in all his days had prepared him for what he was seeing.

The entire world was frosted silver white. What yesterday had been a late autumn meadow was now a frozen mystic wonderland.

Sunrise was still a good half-hour away. Orange and rose hues colored the eastern hills. Each delicate taste of color was reflected in perfect union by the meadow, for the field itself now had no color. Each blade of grass, each tree, every post and thistle and branch was captured by a coat of winter. The white sea was singing in silent unison with the empty sky and the coming light.

A gentle hand rested on his shoulder. Nathan turned to find Poppa Joe studying him with the silent intent of somebody who long ago had learned to look beneath the surface. "First time I laid eyes on you, I thought to myself, now here's a man who'd be touched by the dawn. Ain't many left on earth who know the value of a sunrise." The hand rose and fell. "Glad to know I was right about you, son."

Hurriedly he dressed and followed Poppa Joe from the

house. The old man closed his front door with a simple wooden latch. If there was a lock, Nathan could not see it.

Poppa Joe moved with the stiff angular grace of an aging stork. He picked up each foot and set it down carefully, working his way across the field at a surprising speed. Nathan tried to walk in the old man's footsteps. The silence was so complete, the beauty so perfect, he felt one unwise step might shatter the sanctity of what he was witnessing.

They left the meadow and started up a trail which led them deeper and higher through a steep-climbing forest. The trees were elm and poplar and highland fir, all burdened by their own winter coating. Each leaf was frozen into place, the frost etched in tiny veins across the surface. The pines bore billions of white needles, each one unmoving and breathless with wonder.

They walked long enough for the light to strengthen into morning. Nathan's breath came strong and comfortable, the puffs leading out before him in frosty plumes. The air bit comfortably, the movement warmed him. The boots and the woolen socks gripped the stones, and the old man led him silently onward.

Where the path took a cramped left-hand jink, the trees moved in to embrace him. Nathan found himself pressed up tight against the rock outcrop they were circling.

Then the path straightened, and the trees fell back in unexpected welcome. And for the second time that morning he cried out loud.

The sun had crested the hills to his right, a lancing blade so brilliant it stabbed at his eyes. Before him rested a mountain lake, silver and smoking in the winter morning. The mist rose like beckoning hands, opening to unveil the mystery of every morning, every new beginning.

The light was so intense it threatened to blind him. But Nathan did not want to blink, for fear of losing the image. It was too perfect, too full of beauty to last. He felt the sudden urge to walk out across the surface, to reach into the impossible moment and take for himself a sliver of eternity.

Silently Poppa Joe took his arm, and pulled him around to the right. Nathan let himself be led to a rock that stretched out like a granite throne over the water. He seated himself, feeling the cold bite through his trousers yet feeling that it was right to do so.

Poppa Joe returned with old yellowed newspaper. He motioned for Nathan to rise, and settled it down beneath him. Of course the old man would have something ready. It was only fitting.

He watched Poppa Joe pull two old cane poles from the brush and bring them over, and settle one into his hands. The old man eased himself down beside Nathan, reached into his jacket pocket, and brought out a filthy envelope. With shaking fingers he opened it and scrabbled through the dirt to pull out a couple of worms. Nathan watched as he fitted them on the hooks, and then with the old man he flicked his line out into the water.

They sat like that and watched and shared both the silence and the morning. Nathan was the first to get a bite, and drew in the fish laughing and shouting. For some reason that particular sound was in harmony with the morning, as natural as the silence had been before.

The morning grew brighter and warmer, and the mist evaporated, and the frozen whiteness melted, and the world returned to normal. Of course. Such perfection could not last. Not even here. But for the first time in his entire life, Nathan found himself believing that there really could be some place called heaven.

They caught another three fish before Poppa Joe declared they had enough, that there was nothing like fresh-caught winter trout fried in bacon grease. And Nathan laughed again, feeling a joy he had been sure was lost and gone forever. He felt comfortable with it here, however, even though it was so alien to his world that he could not even name the sensation while it filled his heart. He could not express even his own name just then. But had he been able, he would have said he was snug within this rush of feelings because they were not his, but the morning's.

Nathan did not want to leave. Not even when Poppa Joe rose creaking to his feet and took the cane pole from fingers that had long since gone numb. Not even when Poppa Joe came back from stowing the poles and stood over him for a long moment.

Nathan kept his face turned to the lake, touched now by a

light breeze and by the strength of a real day, and wished there were some way to be the person he was right now for all time.

Poppa Joe eased himself back down beside him, and asked in a voice as quiet as the breeze, "Seems to me you're packing quite a burden, son."

It was perfectly natural to be called son at that moment. Perfectly natural to respond to the comment with a nod. Yes. Quite a burden.

When Nathan did not speak, Poppa Joe did not press. Instead, he used both hands to ease his back, and gave a long sigh. "I was right here on this very spot, when I heard it."

Nathan knew he was being called back from wherever it was he had been. Knew and somehow did not mind. This was the man who had shared his most valuable possession with him. How could he object when he wanted to take it back. Nathan turned to the old man, content to say, "Heard what?"

The clear blue eyes turned Nathan's way. And there in those depths Nathan found himself feeling as though the morning mists had been captured, the mists and all the mysteries they had held, all the secrets.

Poppa Joe finally replied, "I done heard the trumpets of Glory, son. Sat here and listened to their call. Last week it was."

It took a long moment before Nathan realized what he was hearing. "You mean you're sick?"

"Been sick many a time. Being sick is part of being alive." The blue eyes regarded him, unblinking and calm as the day. "I mean I'm dying. The Lord has done called me Home."

Twelve

On that journey, Richmond did not hold its customary charm for Connie. It was an old city, rich in history and heritage, and a welcome change from Hillsboro's confines. If ever Connie were to leave her mountain town behind again, she would have wanted a small apartment in an old house. She particularly liked the area known as Windsor Farms, with its leafy streets and broad sidewalks and southern grace. A little time in Richmond was usually enough to give her a sense of quiet liberation. She could come here and spend a day or so on state business, and return refreshed and ready to constrict herself to the region that was as much a part of her life as the air she breathed.

But not this time.

Her activities were crowded with all she had hoped to leave behind. On Sunday she drove from meeting to meeting, yet heard little besides Dawn's soft questioning tone and the doctor's infuriating ways. She had planned to go see the new film *West Side Story* that evening, since it wouldn't be coming to Hillsboro's only cinema for months. But she had scarcely had the will to eat a bite of dinner before crawling into bed, more exhausted from the internal struggle than from her day's work.

When on Monday she attended the planning sessions with peers from other small towns she heard most clearly her uncle's voice, which was most surprising of all, since Poppa Joe had no place whatsoever in these crowded city scenes.

By lunchtime the voices left her no choice. She excused herself from the afternoon meetings and went back to her hotel room. Before she could argue herself out of what she was planning, she picked up the phone and asked the operator for Baltimore information. She then called the hospital's number and asked for the administrator with whom she had dealt in the past, the only name she could remember without her file.

"This is Margaret Simmons."

"You won't remember me, Mrs. Simmons. My name is Connie Wilkes, and—"

"Of course! You're the city manager of Hillsboro."

"That's a pretty grand title for a paltry town like Hillsboro, Mrs. Simmons."

"Please, call me Margaret. How is Nathan doing?"

Now it was Nathan. She found herself stabbed by confused feelings and became even more cross because of them. "That's actually why I'm calling. We need to talk."

There was a moment's hesitation. "I'm not sure I follow you."

"I'm coming up to Baltimore today. I want to see you."

"I'm extremely busy—"

"Today, Mrs. Simmons. This afternoon. I'm leaving Richmond right now." Connie put down the phone, picked up her purse and case, and headed for the door. It was time for some answers.

When Nathan returned to the clinic on Monday, nothing had changed, yet nothing was the same. The morning light shimmered with the birth of new winter. The air vibrated with the power of all he had experienced. The atmosphere remained dense with the unspoken.

At his request, Poppa Joe was due into town that afternoon. He had refused to come in earlier, saying simply that he had things to attend to, and Duke had agreed to go back up to collect the old man. After the time they had shared, Nathan had found himself unwilling to argue.

It was hard to tell whether the morning cases held more surprises than usual. Or if a doctor more accustomed to general practice would have found them to be surprises at all. For the first time since his arrival, however, Nathan found himself seeing the faces behind the illnesses. Studying the people as well as the complaints. And wondering at the change this represented.

His lunchtime habit was to go directly from the clinic to his home and back, avoiding all contact and holding fiercely to his privacy. But today he found himself letting his feet guide him through the town. The air was soft and cool and scented with coming winter. He could hear the river flowing back behind him, whispering to itself in the distance, full of all the secrets it had carried down from the hills.

Nathan walked down Main Street, not really certain where he was headed, but content to walk and see what came. He felt the looks and heard the cautious distance in the townsfolks' quiet greetings. There was no change in the guarded way they treated him, it was exactly the same as it had been the day before.

Only this day it hurt.

When he spotted the steeple, it seemed perfectly natural that his walk would take him by way of the church. Brian Blackstone was out front tacking green fir and holly branches over the church bulletin board. When he saw who was standing at the edge of the church lawn, he dropped his hammer and walked over.

"It was such a beautiful winter's morning," Brian said in greeting. "I decided it was time to put up a few Christmas touches."

"The radio's been saying the Christmas season has been around for weeks."

"Yes, well, up here we don't always hold to city timing."

"I'm beginning to see that." Nathan searched the brilliant November day for something else to say. The weather was both cold and hot at the same time, as the sun's warmth shared the day with a growing chill. He squinted at the church, built in the same brick-and-stone fashion as his house. "Sure is a pretty building."

"Yes, this style is one of the things I love about our little town. I actually did some research about it. Many of the original settlers came from an area in England where there was a great deal of iron-laced stone. They used it to strengthen their brick structures, because the clay was not of very good quality. Brick-and-flint, the old English houses were called. Most of the oldest Hillsboro buildings were built with that same architecture in mind. Then after the turn of the century, the town became flush with new money, and went on another building spree. Thank goodness they held to the same old style."

"I like it," Nathan said. This was the first time in quite a while he had cared enough to comment on anything beyond the essentials. "The look blends in well with the hills."

"It should. All the materials are native." Brian's gaze held a bit of the same penetrating quality as the old man's. "How was your night up in the highlands?"

The question should have surprised him, but for some reason it didn't. "News gets around fast here."

"That kind of news sure does. Poppa Joe guards his privacy. I can't recall the last time anybody was invited to share an evening with him. And the two of you, well, you've got to admit it makes for a remarkable combination."

The silence lingered as an invitation. Nathan knew he could turn away, and a part of him wanted to leave the questioning and the searching it urged within himself. But he couldn't. He did not know why he felt drawn to the spot and the talk and the man. But he did. "It was . . . mysterious."

He glanced over, ashamed now that he had spoken at all. But all Brian did was nod. Once. A slow up and down, as though the word had registered deep. There was another long silence, then the pastor said, "I find reading the Bible is a good way to put reason behind the mysteries in life."

To Nathan it felt as though this was why he had taken the walk. As though he had been preparing for these words ever since he had left the lake and returned to the valley. Perhaps even before that. Which was why he had the strength to confess, "I've been seeing some cases that concern me."

"Ah." Brian set down his handful of holly and his hammer. "Would you like to come inside?"

"I'd better not." Nathan glanced at his watch. "I need to get back to the clinic before long."

Brian nodded his acceptance. "When I was first starting off here at the church, the old doctor brought me in one day and said that in a town like ours, the doctor and the pastor needed to work hand in glove."

Nathan found himself surprised, not by the words, but rather by his own reaction. Last week the concept would have been reason for scorn. Today it was as natural as this warm-cold light. "There is the problem of doctor-patient confidentiality."

"Exactly what the doctor said. So he made me an unofficial member of the clinic staff. Sort of an unpaid adviser." Brian showed his quick smile. "A lot of people around here take it for granted that their pastor is the one man in town who doesn't need to be paid for extra work."

Nathan allowed his concern to show. "There's a man here in town with a worrying cough. Sounds to me like chronic obstructive pulmonary disease."

"I don't know what those words mean, but I'd guess you're talking about Frank Keegan. Sounds like a cranky cement mixer when he coughs from the back of church."

"Right. According to what he told me today, he's had a productive cough for three months or more every winter for years."

"As far back as I can remember." Brian's smile was easier now, soft as the sun and glowing. "Don't know what I'd do without him hacking to punctuate my sermons."

"You may have to do just that." He said the words with the same cold force he always used for delivering such news. Only this time they stabbed him deeply. "Keegan reports that he's carried this particular cough all summer long."

Brian sobered. "That's right. He has."

"This is not a good sign. It means his lungs have become so weak they can't easily ventilate. The fluids from last winter are still in there." Wishing he could ease back, craving a way to say this more softly. "I'm fairly certain he will succumb to bronchial pneumonia before this winter is out."

Brian turned and inspected the autumn-clad hills. The colors seemed to dance like golden fairies in the mild highland wind. "I've known Frank Keegan all my life. He used to run the soda shop at the other end of town. Spent my first pennies on his cherry pop."

"I'm sorry." Even that came out like a bark. One that had been there for years, only now it sounded alien. Only here it felt all wrong.

Brian sighed. "The hillfolk call chest colds the old man's friend, on account of how it welcomes them into death." He turned his gaze back to Nathan. "Thank you for the news, friend. I will have a word with Frank's family."

Nathan sought for more to say, but could only start for the clinic, shamed by his own failings and scalpel-sharp edges.

"Nathan, wait." When he turned around, Brian asked, "Back to what we were talking about earlier. Would you care to join me for study?"

He managed a nod. Inadequate a response as it was, the movement brought a flash of pure delight to the pastor's features. "That's wonderful, friend. How about tonight after dinner, say about seven?"

"Fine." Nathan walked off, abashed at his paltry wealth of words.

Yet the thought which carried him back to the clinic was of a single word. One twice spoken by the pastor. One which lingered in the air like autumn light, warm and friendly and cool and fresh. He found the word as strange as the comforting silence that held this town, as refreshing as the constant melody the river sang to his approach. Even the rushing waters seemed to echo the thought, the word, the pastor's gift.

Friend.

Thirteen

When Nathan arrived back at the clinic, a lovely blonde woman was leaning over the receptionist desk, smiling and chatting with Hattie. But as soon as his shadow appeared in the doorway, the young lady straightened and the smiles disappeared. The action clawed at him.

"Oh, Doctor Reynolds. Your next patient is ready." Hattie rose from her desk and ran a nervous hand down the front of her dress. "This is my daughter, Dawn."

He could not completely hide his surprise. Hattie was handsome in a strong way, with hollows like windblown hillsides sharpening her face. Dawn was another thing entirely, a truly gorgeous blonde. But her eyes held the level hardness of one long angry. There in her gaze Nathan recognized every brusque word he had spoken to Hattie Campbell.

"The town is surely glad to have you around, Doctor Reynolds." Dawn's voice held the flat quality of a confidence far beyond her years. "Just exactly how long do you aim on staying?"

There it was. The same question he had asked himself so

often. All of the quiet chatter in his reception room halted instantly. The atmosphere condensed into silent waiting.

Nathan took a breath. And it was the breath that saved him. For there in the cramped reception room, filled by worry and illness, he did not smell the age of the house nor the antiseptic cleaner nor the medicines. Instead, he smelled the mountains. And he heard the river, and the mysteries that permeated down from the lake and the hilltop and the frosty winter sunrise to this little room, crowded with people and listening and need.

"I don't know." There was no need for anything except the truth. And the first truth required a second. He turned to Hattie and went on, "I owe you an apology."

His words sounded gruff in his ears. Gruff and holding to the anger that had seen him through so much. Even so, surprise at his words pushed both women back a half-step. "Doctor Reynolds—"

"I've brought a lot of battles up here with me." Strange. Even though the mountain's mysteries remained locked in the realm beyond words and understanding, his own internal struggles were surging forth, forcing him to speak of what he had harbored as secrets for so long. As though the two could not exist within the same soul, the secrets he had brought and the secrets he had found here. "But none of them were with you. I should never have treated you like I have."

"That's right," Dawn said sharply. "You sure shouldn't have. My mama's a saint, and you ought to treat her like one."

Nathan looked from mother to daughter, and for an instant stood at a distance from himself as well. He felt the anger surging, the desire to respond with a blast of his own. But he couldn't. There was a new power there, one which struggled with unseen reins and held him back. He replied, "All I can say is, I'll try to do better."

The room seemed to breathe easier, as though something vital had been witnessed and accepted. The daughter remained unconvinced, her gaze cautious and constrained.

He started to turn away, knowing there was no answer he could give to her original question. Then he remembered and leaned over the desk. He said softly, "Poppa Joe is supposed to come in later."

A hand flew to Hattie's throat. "Oh no. Is there—"

"Just bring him in as soon as he arrives, all right?" He straightened and gave an abrupt nod to the people waiting. There was a quiet murmur of response, the same reserved greeting he met in the town. Nathan opened the door to the back, and wondered how he could feel both enriched and saddened by such a soft little sound.

The day continued at a normal pace. Most of the ailments Nathan confronted were predictable and would heal with time.

He found himself enormously satisfied by this, which surprised him. There was little of the intellectual challenge he had known in the hospital, no sense of pushing forward the boundaries of medical knowledge. He had always considered himself a solid clinician with little ability to deal with patients personally. Yet these people responded to him with trust and almost pathetic appreciation. And addressing complaints which would improve was gratifying beyond words.

Nathan found himself learning from these simple folk, watching their reactions to his words as much as studying their ailments. He did not know exactly what he was seeking, yet found himself comforted to be searching at all. And he saw how most of these people held traces of the same quiet highland strength as Poppa Joe. Softened by life in a town, yet there all the same.

Which was perhaps why he was ready when he opened the door to the rear consulting room and found Poppa Joe seated in the chair by the window. The old man pushed himself erect and said, "Don't look like things is changed much since the last time I was here."

"Medicine has changed enormously. This place is a museum." He shook the coarsened palm, looked around for the file, picked it up, and saw that it was empty. "When was the last time you saw the doctor?"

"Oh, it weren't for me. That was back when my Mavis was feeling poorly."

Nathan set down the empty folder. "How long ago was that?"

"Must be nigh on twenty years now."

"And you've never seen a doctor since then?"

"Nary a time."

Nathan pointed to the examining table. "Sit here on the edge, please. How are you feeling?"

"Not too bad. Few aches and pains. Bit off my feed of late."

Nathan crossed his arms and tried hard to concentrate. Poppa Joe's hand gave palsied tremors as he held the windowsill and settled himself back down. It was a common trait of age, tied to muscle and nerve deterioration. Yet all the medical knowledge in the world could not erase his sudden ache at the thought of Poppa Joe joining the legions of the lost. "Then could you tell me why you think you're seriously ill?"

"I don't think, son. I know." The old man was so out of place here, among the antiseptic smells and harsh clanging sounds and bright instruments. But his blue eyes held the same calm, distant stare. "I'm thinking you ain't a believer."

The quiet statement seemed somehow correct here. "No."

"Well, then. I don't know what I can tell you that you'll understand."

Nathan nodded, aware of how bizarre this conversation would have sounded to his compatriots at the hospital. And yet how natural it sounded here. "Do you have any swellings or discolorations, any unusual pains?"

"Yep. Them I do. But I've had 'em before, mind."

"Well, would you show me what it is you have this time?"

"If'n you want." The old man pushed himself erect and began the laborious process of undoing his shirt. "Ain't gonna do neither of us any good, though."

Nathan resisted the urge to go over and help. "Why did you agree to come in this afternoon?"

"'Cause it was a friend what did the asking." Poppa Joe finished with the last button and pulled off his shirt. "I don't like saying no to a friend."

But Nathan was no longer listening. Even before he had crossed the room, he knew. Before he was close enough to study the discoloration, before he palpitated the skin and noted the lack of normal tension, he was certain.

He eased himself upright, moving as slow as the old man now. Poppa Joe watched him with the calmness of one already aware of what was coming. "I was right, now, wasn't I?"

"I need to get you over to Charlottesville for some blood work and an X ray." He started for the door. "Let me go give them a call and see if they'll fit us in tonight."

"Son?"

But he did not stop. He did not want to answer that question or have his face inspected by those wise old eyes.

His ancient enemy had found him again.

Fourteen

"Mrs. Wilkes? I'm Margaret Simmons." The gray-haired woman approached with a professional smile and an outstretched hand.

"It's *Miss* Wilkes. Connie, actually." Now that she was here, she was nervous. No less determined, but nervous. The woman facing her was impressive. "Thank you for seeing me."

"You sounded very, well, obstinate." The smile was quick but genuine. "I decided it was better to accept than risk losing an argument."

"There are things I need to know," Connie said doggedly. Standing there in the hospital lobby, however, she felt less positive. Everything here was so polished. The place reeked of money and power and knowledge and citified ways. Especially this woman. Margaret Simmons was perfectly dressed in muted tones of cream and ivory and coffee. Her gray hair was fashionably cut, her only jewelry was a watch and a brooch that together probably cost more than Connie's car. The woman stood impossibly erect, and spoke with quick, intelligent bursts. Connie wished she had taken the time to check her makeup. Or that she had not come at all. "We've got a right to know more than you've told us."

"Yes, I see." Margaret Simmons studied her a moment. "Perhaps I was wrong to insist you accept Nathan Reynolds with so little background information."

"Doggone right."

"But you sounded, well, desperate. And beggars cannot always be choosers."

"We may be hard up, Mrs. Simmons. But we're still a town that holds fast to our values and our citizens. We need somebody we can trust."

The gaze remained steady. "You don't find Nathan to be a competent physician?"

"No, it's not that." Again there was the sense of having stepped off into a void. "He's a fine doctor. But he's, he's . . ."

"The most irascible, difficult, stubborn, domineering, extraordinarily infuriating individual you have ever met."

Connie tried to repress the grin, but it managed to slip out of its own accord. "I guess we're talking about the same fellow after all."

Margaret Simmons laughed, and shed both years and her professional barriers. "The first six months Nathan Reynolds worked here, I alternated between wanting to shoot him and wanting to pin a medal on him."

"Which one won?"

"Oh, he was far too talented to shoot. So I just made do by trying to avoid him whenever possible."

"Yeah, that sounds familiar." Connie could not help it. She was finding herself not only outgunned, but actually liking this woman. "I hope it worked better for you than it has for me."

"No, it didn't work at all." She motioned with her hand for Connie to accompany her back through the front doors. "My guess is that a well-run hospital is like a small town in a lot of ways, Miss Wilkes."

"Please, call me Connie."

"And I'm Margaret. A hospital can become a home in and of itself for the dedicated doctor. And there has never been a doctor more dedicated than Nathan Reynolds. At least not one I have met." She led Connie down around the side of the building, following a path which fronted a baffling array of departmental signs. "A good specialist can become so absolutely lost in his work that the outside world becomes a mere shadow. There is a risk in this. A terrible risk, especially if his specialization is one of the, well, one of the more critical ones."

"Nathan's was one of these?"

"Yes," she said, the word a sigh. "Yes, it was."

Connie glanced over as they passed the emergency entrance, with a trio of gleaming ambulances parked alongside.

"It takes almost two hours for the nearest ambulance to get to our town. For the past three years, since our old doctor died, folks with a real emergency got carted to Charlottesville in the back of the town hearse. We always said it was so they could get used to the ride."

"That's terrible."

"Yes, it is. Hard to believe Nathan Reynolds would give up a place like this and start over in our little town."

Lines tightened and lengthened from Margaret's eyes and mouth. "He did not have much choice."

"I'm not following you."

The woman sighed herself to a stop. "There's a similar danger for a hospital administrator. We can come to feel that every day is a battle over money. We can forget we're dealing with lives here. And pain. And fear. And families with hopes and dreams and anxieties that spread out far beyond the confines of our little hospital."

"Not so little," Connie said, wondering at what she was observing emerge in the other woman. "But I hear what you're saying."

"Yes, I believe you do." She gave a quick smile and started off again.

The path led around a protective wall of shrubbery and brought them to a one-story brick building. Its glass entranceway was decorated with smiling suns and huge flowers and children's drawings. In front stood a gleaming jungle gym and seesaw and sandbox. Despite the day's cool sunshine, however, the playground was empty and still. The wind pushed a seesaw back and forth with a dreary squeak. The sight of that silent building and the empty playground drew a shiver from Connie.

"Miss Wilkes, Connie, you have asked me for details about Nathan Reynolds. There is only one way you would understand, and that is for you to walk through those doors. But I warn you, it is a positively terrifying place. I want you to be absolutely sure you are strong enough to learn the answers to your questions."

Margaret Simmons waited, an implacable, determined, very focused woman. Connie looked from her face to the doorway and back again. The desire to turn and run was so great she could actually taste it. She started to speak but halted herself, for the woman's gaze said it all.

She took a deep breath, clenched her hands into tight little balls, and nodded.

"Very well." Margaret Simmons walked over and pulled open the door.

Connie forced herself to enter. The determination that had carried her this far kept her going through the lobby, even though every further step was a struggle. Even though there was no air to breathe inside that large chamber.

The bright pictures and the music and the sunlight streaming through the glass doors did not belong here any more than she did. Nor did the smile which the receptionist gave them. "Mrs. Simmons, what a pleasant surprise."

"Hello, Jill. This is Connie Wilkes. She's city manager of Hillsboro, the town where Nathan is now practicing."

The woman's face brightened even further. "You don't say! How is Doctor Reynolds?"

"Fine." Connie's voice sounded foreign to her ears, shaky and empty. "He's fine."

"Oh, I'm so glad to hear it. He was one of my favorite people."

"Jill," Margaret warned, "come on, now."

"Well, it's true," the woman said stubbornly. "That man was the most caring individual I have ever met, when it came to our children."

A new voice coming down the hallway chimed in, "You can say that again, sister."

Connie turned to meet a large black woman with the same determined strength and intelligence she had found in Margaret Simmons's eyes. "Nathan's working in your town, that what I heard?"

"Yes. Yes, he is."

"Well, you tell him Dolores said we miss him. All of us. The children most of all."

"All right. I will." How could these people be so cheerful? How did they have the strength to come in here at all? It was one thing to walk through those doors the first time. But to do this day after day, how was it possible?

Dolores offered her a warm hand. "Nathan is a gold-plated saint in my book. You can tell him that as well." She gave

Connie's hand a brisk squeeze, then turned away, calling, "I see you over there, Johnny. You hiding from me?"

A young voice said glumly, "It wouldn't do any good if I did, would it?"

"Not a bit. Come on now, the sooner we start, the sooner we finish." She stood and waited for a too-thin waif of a boy to walk over. He had no hair. His scalp was bare save for thin wisps of blond-gray fuzz. He wheeled a metal stand holding a drip attached to his wrist as he walked. The wrist was so thin it made Connie's heart hurt just to look at it. Over in the corner a woman watched the boy walk down the hall with Dolores. A magazine rested opened and unread in her lap.

The receptionist said cheerfully to Margaret, "Anything we can do for you?"

"No, nothing. I just wanted to show Miss Wilkes where Nathan used to work."

Connie wanted to say something. It was only polite. But she could not pull her gaze away from the woman seated in the corner. Her eyes stayed fixed upon the empty hallway, the place where her son had once been. Connie felt if she looked much longer into those red-rimmed eyes, she would never find her way out again.

She started down the hallway because Margaret Simmons took hold of her arm and walked her. "Our hospital is one of four or five in the country to have established such a clinic as this. We specialize in what is coming to be known as pediatric oncology. That is the new medical term for what goes on here. Nathan Reynolds specialized in cancers that attack children. Nathan came here straight from his residency at Sloan-Kettering. He was a prize. Even the senior doctors were amazed at some of the work he did, and those doctors are a hard-bitten lot."

They passed door after door. Connie looked because she could not help herself. Every one of the rooms held a bed and a body too small for the bed. Most of them also held families. All the families held gazes that mirrored the woman in the reception area.

"But Nathan never could learn the vital lesson of separating his private life from his work. He never learned how to walk away and leave this behind, to keep that kernel of spirit and life set apart from what you see here. For Nathan, there simply wasn't anything but work. He gave himself to his patients. Heart and mind and soul."

Margaret Simmons stopped in front of another door. The room held a single bed. An empty one. It should have been comforting to look in that room. But Margaret stared in there with an unreadable expression, and she said, "Oncology is an area of tremendous growth and opportunity. We are making enormous strides. Almost on a monthly basis we are seeing one breakthrough or another." She paused a long moment then, her eyes gazing at the empty bed. "But the fact of the matter is, most of the children who come in here suffer through radical and experimental treatments, and then they die."

The words held such a bitter edge that Connie found herself shivering again. Shivering and sweating at the same time. *Radical.* She could not look at the empty bed any longer.

"Nathan was responsible for two new treatments which have now become standards in the field. He worked not only on healing the children, but protecting them from pain. I can remember some nights, working late, coming down into the cafeteria and finding him poring over reams of scientific journals. And his face . . ."

The hard-edged professional exterior slipped for a moment as Margaret Simmons bit down hard on her lips. There was an instant of waiting, the only sound the murmur of voices from two adjoining rooms. Connie looked away, trying to focus on something, anything else. She found herself reading the signs that marched down the ceiling of the long hallway. Each one of them held such unknown terrors she had to look away.

"His face," Margaret sighed. "His face carried all the pains and the miseries of what he was confronting in here."

Connie wanted to stop the flow. Turn and walk away, or simply say the words, *That's enough*. But she was held by the moment and the place, in a grip as cold and firm as death.

Margaret drew herself upright. "Nathan Reynolds had a nervous breakdown. I could see it coming. All of us could. We tried to talk to him. We urged him to take time off, to go for counseling. We did everything but the one thing we should have done, which was to order him to leave. But the work he was doing, the work . . ."

Then it came. A sound from one of the rooms farther down the hall. A single whimper. A sound as clear as a shattering crystal bell. A voice murmured in response, a man's this time, full of love and pain all its own. And Connie knew if she stayed one instant more in this ward she would go insane.

She turned and started for the doors. She did not care what she looked like, fleeing from the cold shadows that gripped this place and squeezed it dry of air and light and life. She did not care. She had to get out.

She did not stop until the sunlight was bathing her in an elixir she wished she could take and pour straight into her bones. She heard footsteps come up and stop alongside her. She heard the now familiar voice say, "Nathan was in our mental-care facility on and off for eighteen months. When he came out, he was spent. Utterly spent. I brought him home with me for a while. He had become very close to both my husband and me. But Nathan is a doctor. He lives to heal. We had to find some way for him to practice, some place utterly removed from here and everything . . ."

"I understand," Connie said. Finally. And what was more, "I feel like such a fool."

"No, I'm the fool. I made such a botch of this. I tried to correct one mistake by making an even greater one."

Margaret Simmons's hand came to rest on Connie's arm a second time. But now her tone was pleading. "I wanted to give Nathan the chance of a fresh start, do you see? But that was hopeless. I should never have thrust him and his impossible manner into a town of utter strangers, and hope that everything would work out fine. I was blind. Totally blind."

Connie opened her eyes. The light shone down upon them both. The unshed tears in her eyes softened this professional woman, making her edges shimmer and glisten. "You did what you thought was right. What else could you do?"

Margaret started to respond, then stopped herself. "What will you do now?"

"Go home." Connie felt bereft, as though she had lost someone dear to her. She took a breath. "I'm going back to Hillsboro and I'm going straight to Doctor Nathan Reynolds and I am going to apologize from the bottom of my heart."

Fifteen

Nathan found it strange to return to roads that went in a straight line.

He followed the directions to Charlottesville's university hospital. Thankfully the chief resident oncologist had heard of him and his work. Of course they would make time for the patient. Melanoma with possible lymphoma? Critical stages? Could they have a couple of students observe the procedure? Much obliged.

The hospital sat at one corner of the University of Virginia campus, more a part of the city than the university. Nathan had never been there before, but even so there was a sense of returning to his former stomping grounds. As he pulled into the parking lot, he sensed the old surging energy. Simply by being here he was fitting on the familiar armor, hefting the old weapons, returning once more to the battle.

Poppa Joe's reaction could not have been any more different. In the fading light of day his eyes looked washed of both color and certainty. He stood by the car and stared up at the building, and asked, "This thing here, it's important?"

"Absolutely vital."

The old man gazed at Nathan across the top of the car. "Son, you ain't expecting to get me cured in there, now."

"We're here for an examination." He had rehearsed the argument while calling the university doctor. But to his surprise, the old man had fitted himself to Nathan's speedy departure, saying not a word as he had been shepherded out of the clinic and into the car. "We need to have some blood work done and a full set of X rays. We should be finished and on our way back to Hillsboro in a few hours."

He might as well not have spoken. Poppa Joe told him, "Because I ain't worried about going Home. And that's the truth."

"Fine." Nathan came around the car, patted the old man on a shoulder solid as Hillsboro rock. "Let's go get this over with."

As they crossed the lot, Nathan reflected that the air seemed thicker here. Dense and clogged with people and city smells. When they entered the hospital, instantly he was struck by the sharp odors. Poppa Joe stiffened beside him, his eyes open and alert and worried. Nathan gave his name to the receptionist, asked for her to ring the oncology department and let them know they were on their way.

Poppa Joe endured the examination with a detached calm which unnerved even the university specialist. He sat with his shirt off, erect and still while the nurse took blood and the specialist led his students through the cursory inspection.

The three medical students watched with the same kind of avid interest Nathan recalled from his own studies. It was almost a hunger, this desire to study and know and conquer. Only here they were inspecting a new friend. Nathan stood to one side and sensed his own internal fears and shadows congealing into another confrontation with the enemy.

Nathan forced himself to hold steady as the hospital's chief oncologist explained to the students, "Melanoma can be readily identifiable by the black irregular growth you see here below the rib cage. This scab you observe here is also typical, the bleeding lesion which refuses to heal cleanly. Unfortunately it is also extremely aggressive—observe the smaller secondary lesions here on the arm, another there by the collarbone, and here again on the right shoulder."

Nathan remained by the far wall, watching Poppa Joe and finding himself struck by a flood of conflicting emotions. Every professional instinct told him he was acting correctly. Yet there was another voice speaking to him now. One that he had never heard before, not in these surroundings. And that voice left him feeling more ashamed the longer he stood and watched the old man.

"Would you raise your arms, please? Thank you. All right, observe here the protruding lymph nodes. And here, the blue striations, yes, this is definitely more than a simple response to internal infection.

"All right, I will now examine the patient's right hypochondrium. Would you please breathe in for me now?

Good. I am palpating the liver, watch as I press in with my hand, see there? Let out your breath now. Excellent. The liver's edge actually can be felt to slide over the tips of my fingers as the patient exhales. Such swelling of the lymph nodes combined with this enlarged liver definitely indicates advanced secondary metastasization."

The hospital oncologist realized he had been ignoring Nathan's presence, so he turned and invited him to join their group. "Wouldn't you agree, Doctor Reynolds?"

Thankfully, the nurse chose that moment to announce they were ready in radiology. Nathan personally led the old man into the windowless room and stood beside him as Poppa Joe had his first look. The X-ray machine was a huge contraption, one as familiar to Nathan as the back of his hand. Only now he was seeing the apparatus through Poppa Joe's eyes—the steel bed, the empty straps, the cold gleaming overwhelming strangeness.

"They're going to run a solution into your vein. That way we'll be able to see everything with total clarity." Nathan tried hard to sound reassuring. "We'll be as quick as we can."

Poppa Joe allowed himself to be eased onto the metal platform and strapped into place. He answered any question directed his way with solemn courtesy, even addressing the students as *sir.* He did not flinch, not even when the third needle went into his elbow and the nurse apologized for striking the same vein. His gaze remained locked upon the far wall, his expression stern and unmoving. The nurse settled a hard little pillow under his head and asked if he was comfortable.

"Not too poorly, thank you, ma'am. Not too poorly." Poppa Joe glanced at Nathan and added, "But if I didn't know better, I'd say you was fitting me for my box a trifle early."

Nathan moved into the lead-glass booth and watched the students assist the nurse in changing the plates and repositioning Poppa Joe between shots. He recalled the thousands of times he had stood and watched the same process. They were all with him in that moment, all the failures and all the successes. There were very few of the latter.

Afterward he settled Poppa Joe into a padded bench in the waiting area and bought him a soda from the machine. Nathan then followed the doctor into the analysis room. The half-light and the bank of illuminated screens were as familiar as his own hands. The university doctor walked the students through the analysis as the X rays and then the first blood work arrived. Every so often he would turn to Nathan and wait, in case this renowned visitor had anything further to add. Nathan took refuge in silent study of the evidence strewn there before him, feeling utterly helpless and frustrated and lost. A band of steel gradually tightened around his chest, until everything inside his body was being squeezed out. All breath, all hope.

When the analysis was complete and the students had

been dismissed, the university doctor said quietly, "That is one amazing man you've brought in here."

"Amazing is right."

"I have family up on the West Virginia border. That man reminds me a lot of them." The doctor raised his gaze, as if to look through the wall and the distance separating them. "I haven't visited the family in years, strangely enough. They're an uneducated lot, hard to talk with. But I always seemed to leave there feeling ashamed. I suppose it was easier to stay away than figure out why."

The doctor straightened abruptly, realizing what he had just said. He glanced at Nathan, as though expecting to find citified derision. But Nathan met him with silence. The doctor asked, "He a friend of yours?"

"Yes." Nathan felt a sudden burning in his eyes. "Yes, he's my friend."

"I assume you'll want a copy of the plates."

"Please." His voice sounded strangled.

"I'll phone with the results of the other blood work as soon as the lab lets us know." The university doctor offered his hand. "It's been an honor to meet you, Doctor Reynolds." He glanced back at the impenetrable wall. "I'm sorry about your friend."

Sixteen

As they were walking down the hospital corridor, Nathan was suddenly struck by a thought. "I forgot all about Brian."

Poppa Joe followed him over to the pay phone in the hall. "The pastor?"

"I promised I'd come by this evening." When the operator came on, he asked for the number for Reverend Brian Blackstone of Hillsboro. As he waited he went on, "He was going to give me my first lesson in the Bible."

As Nathan fished for change to pay for the call, he glanced up. "What's the matter?"

For the first time that exhausting day, Poppa Joe was genuinely anxious. "I took you away from getting to know the Lord?"

"It's all right."

"No, it ain't." The old man looked stricken. "It ain't all right at all."

Nathan kept glancing over as he waited for an answer. When the pastor came on the line, he started, "Brian, it's Nathan here. I'm so sorry, but—"

The reverend broke in with worry of his own. "How is Poppa Joe?"

"Well, right now he's pretty peeved. He feels like he's taken me away from something important."

"Is he there?"

"Right here beside me."

"Put him on the line, will you?"

Nathan held out the receiver. "He wants to speak with you."

Poppa Joe accepted the phone, bent over to accommodate his height to the short metal cord, and said, "Evening, Reverend."

He listened for a long moment, and gradually Nathan could see the worry creases ease away. "All right, Reverend. I'll tell him. And thankee."

Nathan accepted the receiver, then said, "Whatever you told him seems to have worked."

"Can he hear us?"

"Every word."

"I know you have to protect the patient, but I'm concerned about Connie."

The burden Nathan carried grew heavier. "I agree."

There was a quick intake of breath, then, "It's bad, isn't it."

"Very."

"Oh my, oh my." Brian's voice took on a little tremor. "Look, I just told Poppa Joe that I've been worrying over what to preach on Sunday. It wasn't until I thought about our study tonight that I discovered what was needed for the Sabbath message. And that's the truth."

"Glad to hear it." And then Nathan had an idea. He lowered the phone and said to the old man, "It's going to be so late by the time we get back, why don't you stay down in Hillsboro with me tonight?"

Poppa Joe nodded once. "I'd be much obliged."

When he raised the receiver, he said to Brian, "Could I borrow a set of clean sheets? I've been a little slow with my housekeeping."

"I'll have Sadie go over and air out the guestroom. Drive careful, they say there's going to be a hard frost tonight." The tremor returned to Brian's voice. "You've got a precious cargo there."

When Connie finally pulled into her drive, she was confronted with a familiar shiny red pickup. She groaned her way to a halt, glanced at the clock, and groaned a second time. A bleary-eyed Duke Langdon slid out of the front seat of his truck, and for an instant it did not appear that his knees would support him.

She opened her door and called, "Duke Langdon, are you drunk?"

"No, ma'am. I surely am not."

Then she realized the tall mountain lad had been deep asleep. "It's one o'clock in the morning."

"Yes, ma'am, I reckon you're right."

"Duke." She pushed off the car's lights, got out, and found herself with scarcely the energy left to shut her own door. "Not now. Not you."

"I know. It shoulda been Dawn. But I spelled her a while back. She conked out."

"Not Dawn either. There's not a thing that can't wait until tomorrow—"

"Miss Connie, I ain't here about Dawn and me."

Something in his tone, the way he dragged himself to full alert, brought her up short. "Something's happened to Hattie?"

"No, ma'am. It ain't Miss Hattie." Duke took what appeared to be the hardest breath of his life. "It's Poppa Joe."

Had the car not been there beside her she would have gone down in a heap. "What?"

"I don't know much. Nobody does. But I brought Poppa Joe down to town this morning. I mean, yesterday. Poppa Joe went by the doc's place later. And after that, well, Miss Connie, I'm sorry. I really am." Another tough breath. "The doc lit out of town with Poppa Joe, and they went over to the hospital in Charlottesville."

She forced her legs to straighten and take her back to the car door, though she needed one hand on the hood to guide her. "I've got—"

"They ain't there, Miss Connie. They're back."

"Then I've got to get up the hill—"

"Poppa Joe ain't there neither. I mean, to his place. He's spending the night over to the doc's."

She felt the news spinning her with the fatigue. "What?"

"And far as anybody can tell, Poppa Joe's feeling okay. They didn't say much to nobody. Hattie and Dawn and Sadie Blackstone all went over and cleaned the house real good. That doc, he ain't much for dusting by the sounds of things. They was there when the doc and Poppa Joe came home. The old man looked fine, far as they could tell. Hattie had brought 'em a bite to eat and they set to with a good appetite."

Connie searched the night sky for answers. "Then why . . ."

"Ma'am, I can't tell you a thing more than that. But Miss Hattie, she said you needed to hear from somebody you knew." Duke heaved a sigh. "Sorry it had to be me."

"No, no . . . I suppose . . . Should I go over?"

"Miss Connie, it's one o'clock in the morning, you done said it yourself."

"Yes, you're right, I best let them sleep." But she knew she could not sleep herself. Not now. She looked over at the lanky young man, his face creased by moon shadows. And she said the words because they needed saying. "Thank you, Duke. You've been a good friend this night."

When the sun began scattering soft rose hues over the valley, Nathan climbed wearily from his bed. He had slept less than usual. His night had been spent preparing a plan of attack. It had been a mistake to bring the old man home from the hospital, he knew that now. Nothing definite could be done until the remaining blood work was back, but even so the time could have been used to prepare him for what was to come.

But when he came downstairs, he heard a creaking on his front porch. He opened the door, and found Poppa Joe seated in the one solid rocker, watching the river emerge from the last of the night shadows. Poppa Joe did not turn from his quiet rocking as Nathan walked out on the porch. "You got yourself some rickety furniture here, son."

"I inherited it all with the place." Nathan dragged over a chair he was fairly certain would hold his weight. "Would you like some coffee?"

"Directly. Ain't no hurry. How'd you sleep?"

"Lousy. You?"

"I never was one for lying abed. Got even less use for it as I grow older." The blue eyes finally turned Nathan's way. "Suppose I'll be getting my fill of it and more in the days to come."

Nathan could not sit there like that. The cold was working its way through to his bones. "Let me get on some clothes and heat some water. I'll be right back."

Once inside, he tried to marshal the arguments which had come to him in the night. He ran through everything he would need to shepherd the old man back to the hospital. All the pat answers he had used in the past; the ones to explain how, even though there was not much chance of success, still they had to run a course of treatment. They had to try.

But when he came back outside, Poppa Joe accepted the steaming mug, took a tentative sip, nodded his appreciation of the warmth and the coffee, and said, "Been thinking what it's gonna be like to watch my last dawn."

"We're a way from that yet." But the stout contradiction rang untrue in the frosty morning air. "How do you feel?"

"Same as yesterday, son." Another sip, then he breathed out the words with the steam. "Seen myself some things, I have. Ain't never felt a call to travel much beyond this here valley. But I've come to know these hills. And I love 'em. Yessir, I surely do." Another sip. "I'm gonna miss this part of creation, son."

Nathan sat and watched the old man's stone-carved features take on strength and form with the morning. And everything he had so carefully prepared held to his tongue like glue.

"Spent a lifetime telling myself, where He leads me, I will follow. When He calls me, I will go. But the time's done come, and I ain't ready. I want me some more days tracking game in the hills. I want me some more sunrises. I want me some more time to learn." The hand which raised the mug was shaking harder than usual now. "I'm sitting here seeing the final door right up ahead, and I feel like I've done wasted the better part of every day."

Nathan could not speak. It was simply not possible. There was no space in that sunlit morning for any of the plans and preparations he had formulated the previous night. He sat and sipped his coffee, feeling more helpless than he ever had before. All his weapons had been stripped away. The enemy was going to win. And this time defeat would come without a struggle.

Poppa Joe turned that searching gaze his way. "Gonna need your help with something, son. Connie's not gonna take to this easy. She's not gonna want to hear that my time's come. She's gonna want to fight. She's gonna want to put me in a hospital down there in the city, and let them doctors and nurses grind me down . . ."

For the first time, Poppa Joe's voice broke slightly. He shuddered with all his frame, shaking so hard the steaming liquid sloshed over the side of his mug and ran down his fingers. The shock brought him back from the horror there in his eyes. And gave strength to his plea. "You can't let her do that to me, son. Ain't no way in my state I'm gonna be up to arguing with her. You seen how she is."

"Yes," Nathan sighed. He turned away from the naked fear in the old man's eyes, and watched as the first ray of sun made it over the pass and fell upon the river. The surface sparkled and steamed, throwing up mists and whispers and secrets he wished he could understand. "I've seen how she is."

"I don't want to die in some city hospital, surrounded by all them smells and strangers." When Nathan did not respond, a note of desperation crept into the voice. "I want to live out my days right here in Hillsboro, surrounded by all the things I know and love. Encircled by my friends."

Poppa Joe's tone grated on his raw nerves. Such a strong, good man should never be brought to the point of needing to beg. "I'll talk to her."

Poppa Joe leaned back in his chair, spent from the effort and the fear. "Thank you, son. I do truly thank you."

Nathan remained seated there long after his coffee had grown cold, long after the frost had worked its way deep into his bones. He searched the morning and the river and the mist and the light, but the answers did not come.

Seventeen

He was finally driven upstairs by a need to prepare for the day's clinic. Nathan shaved and dressed with care. As he knotted his tie, he stood studying his appearance. The day called for something more than his customary haphazard attitude toward clothes. But nothing could be done about what stared back at him from the mirror. His face was creased by shadows, some visible and others only he could see.

He inspected his own eyes with a doctor's thoroughness and could not escape the diagnosis. Somehow Poppa Joe's words had robbed him of all his remaining rage. Not just for the morning. For all time.

Accepting the truth in Poppa Joe's plea had meant giving up the struggle—not just for this sick old man, but within himself as well. He was defeated. It was written all over his face. He had nowhere to turn now, not even into fury. All his weapons had vanished. The enemy could attack at will.

Abruptly a sound touched the edge of his hearing, one that startled him so he was drawn from the shadow-born fear. In that instant Nathan thought he heard himself laughing up at the lake. Which was truly bizarre, to stand there confronted with his own impotent sadness, and to remember the happiness of a dawn which seemed a thousand years ago. Nathan turned from the mirror and the memory. And he wondered if he were going insane. Again.

As he came down the stairs, a car pulled into the drive. When he pushed through the front door and saw who was driving, his tie felt as tight as a noose.

Connie climbed from the Olds carrying dark clothes on a hanger. Her eyes looked haunted. "How is . . ." She focused behind him, then forced out a tight smile. "Morning, Poppa Joe. I thought you might want a fresh change of clothes."

"I thank you, daughter." Poppa Joe accepted the hanger. "Sorry you had to go up the hill on my account."

"It wasn't any bother." She leaned forward and gave his cheek a quick peck, then stood watching as he turned and went back inside, the smile straining her eyes and her face.

Nathan tried to hold off her questions with one of his own. "Why does he call you daughter? I thought he was your—"

"Uncle," she finished impatiently, wanting to return to the matter at hand. "After my folks died, Poppa Joe sort of claimed me as his own."

"That's nice."

"He said I was God's gift . . ." The smile almost cracked, but she tightened her face another notch and held to control. "God's gift to a lonely old man."

"I'm sorry, Connie." The shadows he had found in his mirror wrapped their way around the porch and the morning. "I'm so sorry."

Connie let the facade slip away as she grappled for the back of the nearest chair. He moved swiftly, guiding her into one he was sure would hold her weight. She did not shy away from his touch. Once she was seated, he leaned against the porch railing and waited for her to say, "It's bad, isn't it?"

For the first time in his professional life, Nathan had nothing but the bare facts to offer. The words emerged like steam, scalding his own throat. "It couldn't be worse."

"Oh dear sweet Lord." She searched blindly in her purse for a hankie. After a time she managed to say, "You're absolutely certain?"

"The full results of the blood work won't be back until the middle of next week." Even here he could not escape his own need to give her the painful gift of honesty. "But yes, yes, I am. He has what is called metastatic melanoma, as severe a case as I've ever seen. There are additional lesions, suggesting the malignant cells have already spread into the surrounding muscle tissue. There is also evidence he has secondary infections of his liver and lymph nodes."

Nathan wanted to offer her the lie of hope. He wanted to return to the rhythm of tests and treatments. But Poppa Joe seemed to be out there on the porch with them, holding him back, pointing him on the course that seemed to have been chosen by another.

"I should have pushed him to see the doctor sooner. I should have—"

"It wouldn't have done any good. I know this particular

enemy all too well, Connie. Believe me. In a man of his age, the outcome was never in doubt."

Another pause, then, "How long?"

"Hard to tell. I don't know how long he's been ill, you see. This thing could be with us for another six months . . ." He hesitated then. But the gentle push was still within him, urging him on. "But I hope not. For all our sakes."

To his utter relief, his words seemed to resound in her, somehow giving her the power to recover, stop the little gasping sobs, and breathe normally enough to say, "Poppa Joe would hate to go slowly. It would be such a humiliating end."

"He's still so strong, my guess is this thing has come on him very fast. In that case, I'd say the end is going to come just as swiftly."

Then she looked at him, and in the glistening eyes he found the same shadows he had discovered upstairs in the mirror. He wanted to say that he had given them to her, that it was his fault, he had brought these shadows to this little town and poisoned his acquaintances as he had poisoned his own life. But he knew it wasn't so. The same quiet voice, the one he had never heard before in all his days, spoke in that strange silent whisper, and said very clearly that he was there for a purpose. One far greater than anything he could imagine. And the strangeness of this new mystery robbed his heart of the ability to give in to the old dark shadows.

She asked then the question Poppa Joe had dreaded. "Should we take him back to the hospital?"

He squatted down before her, the movement natural, as though he had been doing it all his life. "It wouldn't do a bit of good. And it would do a lot of harm."

Connie wiped the tears from her face, and said quietly, "Poppa Joe would hate it."

"Yes, he would."

"If you're sure it wouldn't help . . ."

"It might delay the inevitable by a month or so. But the stress and the pain, Connie." Nathan stopped then, held by a fleeting series of images. Of families worn to the bone by the battle. "I know this path all too well. This time the battle is lost. I'm so sorry."

She took a deep, shaky breath, wiped her face again, and said the last thing he would have expected to hear. "I visited with Margaret Simmons yesterday."

The words did not strike him as he might have anticipated. They melted into everything else there between them. "Then you know."

"I came back planning to apologize to you. I want to do that, even though . . ."

"Connie, I'm the one who needs to apologize. And not just to you."

There was the sound of overloud footsteps scuffling across the front hall, and a hand fumbling on the knob, granting them time to rise and collect themselves and be ready to meet Poppa Joe with composure as he came through the doorway and said, "Y'all ready to greet the day?"

Eighteen

By the following Sunday, all of Hillsboro knew. At the clinic, in the town, everything continued at its normal pace, and yet everything was changed. Everyone knew about Poppa Joe. One person would ask, the entire town seemed to listen. It was that way. Hillsboro became a waiting room filled with bereaved relatives. Even the simplest word bore a shared concern.

That morning, as Nathan was relishing the late winter sunrise and his first cup of coffee, Connie called. "I hope I'm not disturbing you."

"Not at all." Which was not exactly true. The jangling phone had set his heart to racing. He had not received more than two dozen calls his entire time in Hillsboro, almost all of them emergencies. "What can I do for you?"

"Poppa Joe came down the mountain this morning. He's here with me now."

"How is he?"

"Fine. He's . . . fine."

"Connie, you need to be sure and tell me if he starts feeling pain." No need to say it was an almost inevitable result of Poppa Joe's illness. No need at all. "I can help with that."

"Yes, thank you, I will. But that's not . . . Actually, I'm calling for him."

"Oh." He finally understood. "Can he hear us?"

"Every blessed word." She sounded stiffly formal. "He doesn't take to telephones. He's asked me to call and see if you wanted to join us for church."

Nathan found himself comfortable with the idea. More than that. It felt *natural.* As though church were just another part of whatever was happening in him, and in his life. "Sure."

Connie hesitated. "You mean it?"

"Be happy to."

"Well, great." She brightened perceptibly. "I'll be by to pick you up in fifteen minutes."

Connie took the long way to church, such as it was. Nathan sat in the passenger seat and watched the little town roll by. The hardware store, the livery stable converted into Campbell's Grocery, the barber shop with the honest-to-goodness red-striped pole, the pharmacy with the soda fountain running alongside the window. The post office with the empty flagpole. The gun and fishing supply store. The farm supply store, its lot of tractors and agricultural equipment forming a triangle between Main Street and the county road. Connie turned back there, doing a second sweep down Main. Poppa Joe sat in the back seat, taking it all in with his customary silence, his eyes glued to the window.

From Main, Connie wound her way through the town's oldest neighborhood. Most of the homes were turn-of-the-century brick-and-stone, sheltered by ancient fruit trees and hardy dogwoods. Front porches were broad and welcoming, rockers and swings and hickory chairs settled in place and ready for company.

The steeple rose above the poplars and old oaks, high enough to catch the fleeting clouds. Connie parked in one of the reserved spots near the front entrance. Nathan climbed from the car in time to see Connie resist her urge to help Poppa Joe. The old man rose to full height, and joined the hills in their solid worth. He wore a shiny dark suit and the first string tie Nathan had ever seen outside the movies. On him it looked perfect.

There was a crowd gathered on the church's front lawn. All faces turned at their approach, imperfect mirrors reflecting varying degrees of what the old man carried with him so naturally. Their greetings were quiet and careful, the faces saying plainly that they had heard the news.

Hattie walked over and stopped their forward progress by giving Connie a long hug. Their faces looked like two sides of a coin, different and yet holding to the same strength and grim sadness and love. Hattie moved back and her place was taken by the lovely young blonde woman. Dawn did not clasp Connie for as long; it was all she could do to hold back the tears.

Neither of the women hugged the old man, but the looks

they gave him were full of love. Poppa Joe responded with grave nods, the occasional how-do, and continued his solemn tread up the stairs and into church.

On into December, visits to Connie's home became how Nathan measured out his days. Poppa Joe had silently accepted Connie's insistence that he come and live with her. Now that he had won the right to finish his days there in the valley, the where and the how seemed to matter less and less.

Nathan's mornings began with a drive down sleepy silent streets, savoring the mist which descended on many nights to drift in lazy frozen curtains along the valley floor. Nathan loved these times alone with the town. During those drives he could almost imagine himself spending his entire life there, allowing the town and the valley and the mountains and the mystery to work its way deep inside his very soul.

Mysteries. They drifted with the fog on such a morning as this. The sermon he had heard that Sunday, and those from the two Sundays before, melted and flowed together. He thought often of the words. So often, in fact, that much of what he experienced and endured during those days was granted definition by the sermons. And comfort. Which was the strangest thing of all, because those Sabbath lessons contained a challenge which threatened to redefine his entire life.

That day, a frozen still Friday in the middle of December, Nathan found himself driving through the quiet streets paying more attention to the words in his head than the journey. The road had become comfortable by then, the town's quiet so familiar that it was hard to remember how he had ever been easy with anything else. The winter morning seemed illuminated by the words of the sermon which drifted through his mind. Nathan found himself able to hear the pastor and his lessons and his challenges more clearly here and now than when he had been seated inside the church.

"Sadly, we spend most of our lives feeling as though we are stuck in a hole," Brian Blackstone had said the previous Sunday. "Life and circumstances are piling up, problems are pressing down, and all we can hope is simply to make it through this one day. Day after day, we are pinched and pressed and battered by the harshness of our lives. Faced by pressure points, unable to see how we are to deal with our problems. Or, even worse, how we are to deal with our fears.

"Fears *attack* us. They grant our memories such power, such force, that we feel we are being assaulted both by the past *and* by the present. We have so many experiences of fear. So many uncertainties of life. So many impossibilities, so much we cannot see our way through. So many things we cannot handle on our own. So many burdens from our past, which crowd up whenever we encounter problems in the present. So many fears of the unknowns still ahead.

"How does a person come through these things intact?

How does a person heal the past wounds? How does he prepare for the future? The answer, my friends, lies in accepting that alone we cannot. Alone we will fail. Though we might win in one instant, though our strength could be enough for one moment, in the end we will be brought down in failure. We will fade, we will pass on, alone, desolate, defeated. Alone, there is no answer.

"But today we are here because we know that we are *not* alone. Our gathering is a divinely inspired assembly, and in our joining we declare this to be holy ground. The very moment is holy. We are not here by chance or choice. God has created a moment of appointment with Him. We call this holy encounter the Sabbath worship. The intent is that here in this moment, our lives will be touched by the Word, by the Truth. We therefore ask for the Spirit to reach into this gathering and have an impact upon this worship, upon this moment, and upon our lives. We ask to be enriched with the power to raise us above our fears, to give us a healing from our past, and bring us to eternal victory."

The request for internal enrichment had not been answered then, at least not that Nathan could tell. But now, as he drove through this misty valley sheltered by frost-covered hills, he felt a shielding so strong it granted him the freedom to look without pain at himself and his life. It was a remarkable experience, a liberating force.

When he arrived at Connie's house he stopped in the street, for the gravel drive was filled by a wrecker cranking up the front of Poppa Joe's truck. He got out and walked over to where Connie stood standing alongside, tears streaming down her face.

She looked up at him and whimpered, "It feels like everything good in my life is just fading away."

"Now don't you worry none, Miss Connie," the mechanic called over. "Morning, Doc."

"Good morning." The mechanic was a man Nathan knew vaguely from church. On the wrecker's grease-streaked door was the name of Allen Motors, the Ford dealership owned by the mayor. "What's the matter with the truck?"

"Reckon it ain't nothing but age, Doc. And it ain't nothing we haven't done over before." He stopped the grinding winch and started back toward his door. "We'll have the old lady right as rain soon enough, Miss Connie. You'll see."

Connie watched him climb up in the cab, then stared forlornly at the ancient truck and asked, "But for how long?"

It was the most natural thing in the world to settle his arm on her shoulders and steer her back inside the house. Nathan stopped where the trellis reached out and enfolded the top of the banister. Tiny champagne roses hung dried and frozen upon the winter-clad vine. Great windows emerged from the blooms like happy faces dressed in sweet-scented veils. "Have I ever told you how much I like this house?"

The statement was enough to give her sadness pause. "Not that I recollect."

"It's very feminine. Which is a strange thing to say about a house of brick and stone. Is it old?"

"Not hardly." Connie paused on the top step to wipe her cheeks. "About fifteen years ago the county bought what was left of our family's bottom land to straighten the state road. I used the money to build this place."

The roof was angled over three ledges like a Dutch barn. The second floor windows emerged from porticos broad enough to permit space for bright yellow latticed shutters. The trellis and its heavy layer of flowers opened around the same yellow shutters for each of the great downstairs windows. "You did a fine job."

"I got the idea from a picture in a magazine. It's sort of copied after a cottage in the French countryside." She looked around, taking strength from the home and the morning. "I guess I was being silly over that old truck, wasn't I?"

"Not at all." Nathan still held on to her arm. He liked the way it felt, grasping this strong yet feminine lady. "It's perfectly natural. Don't be too hard on yourself."

"Right. Why bother, when so many others are willing to be hard for you." But the attempt at joking fell as flat as her sigh. Connie turned around and said, "Poppa Joe's been asking for you."

This was not good. "Is he in pain?"

"Not that you'd know. But then, he's never been one for complaining."

Together they passed through the living room. Connie

had collected crystal-bearing rocks from different places along the Appalachian Trail, and set them so sunlight entered the tall windows and turned the ceiling into a collection of rainbows. But not today. The gray mist gathered around the windows, and even an hour after sunrise she still needed the lamps.

The hallway had long since become crowded with all the odors of the seriously ill. Nathan found the familiar scents oddly jarring here, in this home with its veil of blooming flowers and its quiet orderliness. Even in winter, when the earth was frozen and the sky quiet, the odors here seemed a violation of this woman's determined strength.

As he walked down the back hall a voice called feebly, "That you, son?"

"Good morning, Poppa Joe." He entered the back bedroom, his eyes adjusting swiftly to the gloomy light. Recently the old man had become sensitive to anything but the dimmest illumination. "How are you feeling?"

"Right poorly."

The quiet admission brought a startled frown to Connie's face. Nathan could well understand. The old man never complained. Never. Even as the illness devoured his strength like locusts going through a field of ripened corn, even as his flesh wasted away until his skin lay flaccid upon his frame, Poppa Joe refused to complain.

Connie dropped down beside the bed. "What's the matter? Why didn't you say something?"

"Oh, it ain't my body, gal. I'm not any worse today than yesterday." And it seemed true, for his voice still held its quiet strength. And his eyes remained unglazed. This was one of the high points of Poppa Joe's day, when the medication that saw him through the night had worn off, and the pain had not yet set in. He and Nathan would sit a while, perhaps talking, more often just sharing the morning quiet.

Then he would stir, or grimace slightly, and Nathan knew that the tentacles of discomfort were spreading. After he had sent the old man off again into a dull-eyed comfort zone, Nathan found himself spending the entire day looking forward to the next few minutes when he and the old man would sit together that afternoon, alert and listening to all that went unsaid.

Connie seemed to release herself from the chains of tension. Now that she was sure he was not suffering, she allowed herself to glance at her watch. "I'm already late for work. Dawn promised to be back here in half an hour, Poppa Joe."

"I'll stay until she arrives," Nathan assured her, and settled into the chair by the bed.

Connie looked down at him, and for a single instant allowed her own veils to fall. Her gaze was full of shattered dreams, until they too fell away to expose a heart full of longing. And something more. But all she said was a whispered, "Thank you."

She leaned over to kiss her uncle's forehead. Poppa Joe responded with a murmured, "Take care, daughter."

After she had gone, they sat there in the silence. It was Poppa Joe's natural state and was becoming increasingly comfortable to Nathan. Every once in a while he would glance over. The old man lay there, all but gone save for the light in his eyes and the rasping strength in that voice.

But today, somehow, the silence was not enough. Nathan cleared his throat and said, "Sitting here with you, I feel a remarkable sense of refuge."

Poppa Joe strained to turn his head so that the gaze could lock in on him. "I'm comforted to hear that."

"It's crazy. I've spent all my life fighting cancer. The enemy. That's how I've always thought of it. And yet here I am, sitting helpless, watching you die, and I feel comfortable." He shook his head. "I must be crazy."

"Don't sound that way to me." The old man weakly cleared his throat. Nathan had come to know the sound and the message, and reached for the frosted pitcher of ice water. He poured a glass and held the straw to Poppa Joe's mouth, then set the glass back down. Poppa Joe went on, "You recollect us talking about how folks used to call the local doc the Gatekeeper?"

"I remember."

"Well, sometimes a man's task is to accept God's will. Hard thing to do when our will is different. But a strong man, now, he learns to accept what he can't change."

"My whole life has been spent pushing back the borders of death."

"That's good, son. But a man's days are measured. Sooner

or later, he's gonna face that door. The question then is, will there be folks there to help give his passage dignity?"

Nathan found himself having difficulty swallowing. "You're the one with dignity, Poppa Joe. You give it to everybody around you."

The old man did not respond for a long moment. Finally he went on. "Been laying here thinking for quite a spell. Found myself able to look on up ahead. The door's right there in front of me. Ain't able to hear the Lord call my name yet, but I know He will. Yessir, He surely will. And soon."

In the gaunt face with its bones punched upward like stones in a wind-carved cliff, the eyes burned bright as spotlights. "Got myself in a muddle, son. Think maybe you could help me?"

"If I can."

"I been laying here wishing there was some way to make my passage mean something."

"I'm not sure I follow you."

"Just wish I could carry something with me. A parcel of good I could take with me up to the high place and set down there before the throne." He held Nathan with a gaze as powerful as a vise. "Something worthy to give my Maker. And I got myself the feeling you're the only one who can help me do it."

Nathan felt the words merge in his heart with those spoken by the pastor. He wanted to object that he had little to offer anyone here on earth, much less to a God he was only now coming to think might exist at all.

But before he could form the words, Poppa Joe halted him with a grimace. Instantly Nathan reached for the bottle and the syringe. That twitch of the face was Poppa Joe's only signal that the pain was growing intolerable. Nathan inserted the needle into the vein, pressed down the plunger, and watched as the gaze dimmed and the eyes closed. Then he sat there, listening to Poppa Joe's weakened breathing, and pondered on what the old man had just said.

Nineteen

The voice, when it came, seemed to bring Nathan out of an open-eyed slumber. "Are you gonna sit there all day?"

Nathan raised his gaze to where Dawn stood standing in the doorway. "How long have you been there?"

"Oh, hours and hours." She smiled at him, her head cocked so that the blonde hair spilled over one shoulder. "You know what? You looked like Poppa Joe just then."

"It must be the gloom." He glanced over at the bed. The old man was resting peacefully. Nathan pushed himself to his feet. He had been sitting in one position so long his legs tingled. "I better be getting off."

"I mean it, you had that same look he gets when he stares off into space and the whole world just fades away." Dawn looked past him to the bed, and her smile turned sad. Nathan watched her face and saw how she was busy putting all she said into the past tense. "Don't know what I'm gonna do without Poppa Joe Wilkes." She drew a broken breath. "This town ain't gonna be the same without him around."

He nodded, and felt the need to speak, to force her to begin preparations. *Gatekeeper.* "It won't be long now, Dawn."

The words coursed through her with trembling force. She gave a tiny nod.

Nathan set a hand on her shoulder, as easy as he had with Connie, then walked out of the room and down the hall and into the gray-clad day. As he climbed into the car and started the motor, he thought he heard Poppa Joe's voice again, speaking of yet another mystery. No matter what his logical mind might say, Nathan felt as though the man had settled an obligation upon his heart.

That afternoon Connie was watching a state crew dig a hole alongside the county road when Brian Blackstone's car pulled over and stopped. Connie stepped away from the men and their machinery and met him as he opened his door. "Don't tell me the church has lost its water too."

"Not so far as I'm aware." He smiled at her. "How are you, Connie?"

"Coping." She stared back at the hole in the ground. "I never thought I'd be glad for a problem with the water lines, but right now anything that gets me out of the office is a blessing."

"You look tired," he said, and motioned for them to walk further away from the ditch digger and the men. "Are you sleeping?"

"I lie in bed a lot. I close my eyes. I suppose there must be some sleep in there somewhere." She huffed a sigh, wanting to do away with such talk. "How are Sadie and the baby?"

"Both are doing just fine." He had aged well, the pastor, despite his own hard times. His face retained its boyish soft angles and gentle look, his eyes remained clear and alert. "I've been worried about you."

"You shouldn't be. I'll get by."

"Life isn't about just getting by, Connie." When she did not respond, he went on, "You're the hardest kind of person to reach. You come to church, you study, you pray, you go through all the right motions. But when a crisis strikes, you don't want to admit you need more help than what is available."

"You and your fancy speech." But her scoffing lacked conviction. "I don't have a crisis, Brian. I have a sick uncle."

"Connie," he started, but sighed himself to a halt. "Call me if you need me, all right?"

Connie stared after him as he turned and walked back to the car. She had never gotten off so lightly with the pastor before. It left her more uneasy than an argument.

That night, the inner voices and the worries and the sense of life unraveling filled the dark corners of Connie's room. They did not so much permit her to sleep as push her into confused slumber and draw her back again, almost against her will.

She awoke to a sense of having heard something, yet the house and the night were utterly still. More than quiet. The air seemed close, like the gathering pressure that came before a summer storm. And yet, as she rose from her bed and slipped on a robe, she did not find it uncomfortable. Just odd.

The gathering stillness accompanied her down the hall to the back bedroom. Quietly she pushed open the door and stood there listening for a moment.

A voice from the bed rasped, "That you, daughter?"

"Are you all right?"

"Couldn't sleep."

She reached behind her and snapped on the hall light. A faint yellow glow revealed Poppa Joe settled in his bed, his eyes awake and watching her. She asked, "Are you in pain?"

"It's been a hard night," he admitted.

"I can give you an injection." Connie opened the drawer to his bedside table. "Nathan showed me how. He said there might be a time—"

"That Nathan is a fine fellow." Poppa Joe followed her with his eyes as she pulled out the little metal box with its implements. "Troubled, though. Man's had himself a hard row to hoe."

Connie fitted the needle onto the syringe, and unscrewed the top from the vial. "Did he tell you that?"

"Didn't have to. I asked him if he wanted to share his burden. He wasn't ready." His eyes were on her face now. "He's gonna need a hand to find his way, daughter. Got to learn how to open up and get that load off his heart."

She filled the syringe to the point Nathan had indicated. She pulled the needle out of the rubber stopper. "I like him," she confessed quietly.

"I'm glad you do, darling. He needs your strength."

She stopped what she was doing and looked down at Poppa Joe. "He also makes me madder than a hornet on a hot August day."

"That's natural enough. You're both too good at being alone."

"And just exactly what do you mean by that?"

Poppa Joe stared at the ceiling. "I figure that Nathan is near 'bout the strongest man I ever met, in his own way. Problem is, he don't know it. All he can see is his burdens and his woes and his failures." The old man was silent for a time, his breath rasping harshly in the night. Then he said, "Man's got two problems. He don't know he's strong, and he can't find his way."

Connie set the syringe down carefully on the towel laid across the top of the bedside table. "I don't think I could help him find that out. I don't hardly know it for myself."

"Oh, you know, child. You just forget sometimes. We all do, when times is hard and the Lord seems distant." He kept his eyes on the ceiling, as he went on, "No, that man's got to let the Lord show him the way, plain and simple."

She opened her mouth to speak, but something halted her. There was a sense of gathering. She had no other way to describe what she felt. A gathering of the night's silence, a sense of gentle power moving into the room. The hall light seemed to reach out further and further, until even the night itself was pushed from the room. It raised the hairs on the back of her neck, but she was not frightened. The presence was too gentle to be threatening.

"I feel like I've let God get too far from me."

She had not even realized she had spoken until she recognized the voice as her own. It was as though the words had sprung from a place so far inside her that they came from beyond herself. She looked down at Poppa Joe, but he continued to stare at the ceiling, his gaze centered on something only he could see.

She heard him say, "Knowing a problem takes a body halfway to solving it."

She inspected him, wondering if he felt it too. But his breathing remained unchanged, each breath drawn with an effort that registered on his wasted features. Yet his eyes shone with the same light she felt building in the room, pressing in on her heart.

"I asked Nathan if he'd help me with a problem. One that's been worrying me something awful." Poppa Joe paused long enough to lick dry lips. Connie reached for the glass and fitted the straw into his mouth. His swallows sounded strangled. But when he had finished, he spoke with the same calmness as before. "I told him I've been wanting for something I could take with me. Something I could lay down before my Lord. Something that'd give my death meaning."

She wanted to tell him to not speak of his dying. But the gentle power would not let her. Instead, she had the sense of her heart being pointed toward what Poppa Joe had just said, as though here were both a mystery and a key. And a challenge. She found herself shivering slightly as she sat there and listened as Poppa Joe's breathing gradually eased, and the eyes closed, and the old man drifted off into slumber. The presence in the room seemed to back away, out of the chamber and down the hall and away from the house, allowing the night to return. Still she sat there, feeling the words ring deep inside her. And she wondered how losing Poppa Joe could ever have more meaning that it already did.

Twenty

On Friday morning, the week before Christmas, Reverend Brian Blackstone stopped by the clinic. In the days and weeks to follow, the visit became fixed in his mind as the moment when he realized change was coming to Nathan Reynolds.

As soon as he entered the clinic, he could not help but notice the differences. For one thing, Hattie Campbell was smiling. Fresh flowers stood in a vase on her desk. A pile of new magazines replaced the dusty copies of *Family Circle*. The locals who sat there chatted quietly, their manner easy. Illnesses were compared, especially by those bringing children, and recipes exchanged.

"Hello, Brian, how are you?" Nathan Reynolds came through the doorway leading to the consulting rooms, his arms full of files. He set them down on Hattie's desk and walked over. His nod to the waiting room was relaxed. "Nothing's wrong with Sadie or the baby, I hope."

"No, they're both fine." Brian felt the eyes, knew all were listening carefully. "Actually, it's about one of my other parishioners."

"Well, come on back." The doctor's voice was different too. Not a smile, no. But no hostility either. The doctor looked tired and drawn, but what doctor didn't. He gave the room another brisk nod. "Won't keep you folks long."

Brian waited until they were in Nathan's office and the door was closed before observing, "You're going through some changes of your own, Nathan."

"Yes, I suppose I am." He had the doctor's air of pressures on all sides, yet focused tightly upon the moment at hand. Like a dark-haired cat resting with weary vigilance behind his desk. "What can I do for you?"

Brian found himself picking his way delicately through unfamiliar territory. "As much time as you've been spending over at the Wilkes recently, have you noticed any changes in Connie?"

"She doesn't appear to be doing too badly, considering the fact that she's losing her uncle."

"She's losing more than that. Poppa Joe is her last living relative, as far as anybody knows. And somewhere in the process, she also appears to have lost her snappish nature."

Strong features stretched in a quick flash of humor. "I'm not sure I'd miss that so much."

"You would if it meant the heart was going out of her." Brian knew there was no way to express his worries. All he could do is plant the seeds of concern. "Connie has been a bedrock of this community, as much as Poppa Joe in her own way. She's the one who looks out for our interests when it comes to competing voices in the county and state governments. She's as fiercely protective of this little town as a mother hawk is over her brood. At least, she was."

Nathan pondered the news. "I'm not sure I understand what you want me to do."

"You're with her a great deal. So are Hattie and Dawn, of course, but they're too caught up in losing Poppa Joe to notice the noses on their own faces. I'd just be grateful if you'd keep an eye out for Connie. Make sure she gets some rest. Tell her to get out a little. And if you see anything alarming . . ."

"I understand." Nathan seemed ready to rise and cut off the discussion, pulled by all the people waiting in his front room. Then he reconsidered and settled back. "The whole town is taking Poppa Joe's illness very hard."

"This is going to be the most somber Christmas I've ever known," Brian agreed, aching from the coming loss. "It's like the heart is being torn from the town's chest."

"I don't have a single patient in here these days who doesn't mention something about the old man."

"Poppa Joe is the essence of what we hold most dear." Brian struggled to tell this newcomer what was so close to him he did not even think of it very often. "He's the last of a very special breed."

"The morning we were up there together . . ." Clearly Nathan fought against the same inability to place the inexpressible into words. "I feel like it marks the beginning of a, well, maybe a new page in my life."

Brian found himself feeling closer to the man at that moment than ever before. But all he said was, "I think I understand."

Nathan glanced at his watch and rose to his feet. As Brian followed him to the door, he went on, "Last week Poppa Joe asked me something that's kept me up nights. He said he wanted to give his death meaning. Said he wanted something he could take up with him."

"What do you think he meant?"

"I . . . " Nathan walked him down the hall, then hesitated at the waiting room door. "I've been thinking a lot about your sermons."

"There's only one greater compliment you could give a minister than to say his sermons have made you think."

But Nathan was too caught up in his own thoughts to ask what that other compliment might be. "Sometimes I feel as though the answer is there in what you've been saying. If only I could work my way deeper, understand things better."

Brian sensed he was bridging a chasm as he reached over and patted the doctor's arm. "Any time you feel like stopping in for a chat, feel free."

"Let's do that next week," Nathan said, opening the door and offering Brian his hand. "Thanks for coming by."

Brian smiled his way through the waiting room and walked back into the morning.

Hattie followed him out the clinic's front door and stood

there on the little porch beside him. "What's got you smiling so?"

He cocked his head to inspect the surrounding hills. There had been no snow so far that winter. Each time the clouds had moved in to blanket their valley the temperatures had warmed, so that even the high reaches had remained brown and bare. "I'm almost afraid to tell you, it's such a fragile thing."

Hattie crossed her arms. "You can't say that and not say more. I'd burst from curiosity."

Brian took a breath of crisp winter air, listened to the river whisper its constant melody, and felt as though his heart were growing wings. "Back in there, I had the strongest feeling that we've got ourselves a new doctor."

Twenty-One

On Saturday Nathan completed his half-day clinic by lunchtime, wished Hattie and his final patients a good weekend, locked the front door, and returned to his office. Nine weeks in the place was enough to consider it his office, not the old doctor's. Some days he could even keep from growing furious over the state of the old place. At least for a while.

Nathan no longer needed to check his book for Connie's number. When her voice came on the phone, he asked, "How is Poppa Joe?"

"Resting comfortably." She sounded more than weary, just as Brian had described the day before. Her words hung as limp as fresh wash on the line. "He managed a few steps this afternoon, and he had lunch with me in the kitchen. What little he ate, that is."

"That's very good." Nathan had come to know a lot about this strong woman during the past weeks. The resignation had been building, he knew it now. Only it had been easier for him to pretend not to notice. "Are you there alone?"

"Unfortunately." The question seemed to threaten her with weary tears. "Hattie and Dawn are off looking at wedding dresses."

The Campbells had been spending more and more time with Connie. Seldom did she spend the night alone with Poppa Joe. Nathan asked, "Someone is getting married?"

"Dawn. That's another mess I've gotten myself into. Hattie is my oldest and dearest friend, and Dawn is like a daughter to me." But the statement only increased her misery. "Oh, I'm so alone."

"Connie, you have more friends than anybody I have ever met." He felt his heart go out to this strong handsome woman in her moment of weakness. "Look, why don't you and I go out for dinner?"

That brought a little choking laugh. "You must be kidding."

"Why do you say that?"

"You want to take me out? After the way I've treated you?"

He smiled into the receiver. "I'd say we were running pretty tight for first place on that score."

Connie murmured, "Goodness only knows I could use a night away from everything."

By the time they had finished making plans, an idea had begun germinating in Nathan's mind. One that took him out of the clinic and started him through town. There were a number of places in Hillsboro which lay somewhere between a too-short drive and an over-long walk. He usually let himself decide by whether he could tie the task in with others, so that he would stop several places along the way. Today, however, he just felt like walking.

The morning mist had not cleared with the day. Instead, the clouds had thickened until they rested like a dark gray ceiling over the entire valley. Hills rose to either side, locking the town in with brown-green walls. On such a day as this, Nathan could well understand the locals' desire to occasionally escape into the flatlands and the cities.

Season's greetings were called to him from almost every door along Main Street. Nathan did not stop, however. He had learned that the words were not demands, but rather invitations. It was his choice whether or not to respond.

There were signs of Christmas everywhere, from bunting strung along wires crossing Main Street to the plastic candy canes adorning telephone poles. Shop windows were framed in fake frosting, and displays held a seasonal motif. Yet it all lacked the overbearing quality of a big-city Christmas. The frenetic energy, the clamor to buy and do and rush and go, all of it was absent here. Nathan walked under the lowering sky, feeling at ease with himself and the place and the time.

He did not know when the change had started, but the evidence was everywhere. It could not be denied. Somehow Poppa Joe's illness had carried with it a healing of his own relations with the town and the folk.

It left him thinking back on their talk of several mornings ago. Nathan found himself wishing there were some way to unlock his stubborn resolve, release the mystery, and do what he knew the old man had requested. But a lifetime of fighting alone left him pounding a mental fist against a tightly locked door.

His way led him down to where Main Street made its northern connection with the county road. Allen Motors occupied the corner lot, anchoring the town to progress and the road ahead, just as the southern post was held by a company selling farm machinery. Fuller Allen's dealership also had the Esso franchise, and the agricultural place sold Sunoco.

"Well, hey, Doc!" The town's portly mayor stepped from the tiny glassed-in Ford showroom and came beaming over. "Just what I like to see, a customer arriving on foot."

"I'm not a customer, and I'm on foot because I felt like walking." But Nathan's tone lacked its former bite, and both men knew it. Nathan accepted the handshake. "How are you, Mayor?"

"Fuller's the name, and I'm fine as I can be in the middle of winter without a sale this week." But his smile didn't slip. "This a social call, or am I sick and don't know it yet?"

"You're fine, far as I know. I came to ask about Connie's truck, the Hudson Terraplane."

The smile finally faded. "Come on around back."

The three bays were all full. "Selling gas and servicing old cars, this is what we live from," Fuller said as they entered the garage. "Folks 'round these parts don't buy a new car unless the last one has given up the ghost, rolled over, and begged for a decent burial."

The mayor directed him over to what was probably intended as a spare-parts bay. "We've been tinkering on it a little now and then, mostly just so I wouldn't have to lie when I tell Connie we're doing all we can." He stopped in front of the ancient truck. "Earl, come on over here a minute, will you?"

"Sure, boss." The wrecker driver ambled over, gave Nathan a grease-stained wave. "How-do, Doc."

"Doc here wants to know about Poppa Joe's truck."

"Aw, there ain't much wrong with this thing except it's just done got old." The man was all gangly angles and sharp edges. He leaned one blackened hand on the truck's fender and peered under the hood. "Reckon I'll be able to patch it together one more time."

"Earl's been servicing this truck for, how long is it now?"

"Shoot, must be going on sixteen, seventeen years. Since my first winter on the job." He gave the doc a gap-toothed grin. "Know this truck better'n I know my littlest one."

"Earl's problem these days is parts."

"Got me a feller down Roanoke way," Earl agreed. "He's started making me parts by hand I can't find nowhere else. But he's getting on, and I don't know anywhere else to go."

Fuller gave his jowls a somber shake. "Hate to be around whenever Connie hears Earl can't keep that truck on the road."

"Lady's sure attached to this old heap," Earl agreed. "Hate to tell you, but the end won't be long in coming."

Nathan moved over to one side and inspected the vehicle. He found himself recalling earlier days, poring over truck books and magazines. His childhood hobby had later become his one escape from the world of medicine. "But is the chassis still sound?"

"Shoot. This here Hudson was made from the finest steel going. Solid as a rock." Earl laid a possessive hand on the fender. "Connie's problem is money. She wants me to repair what's got it off the road, nothing more. I keep telling her she needs to take care of all the little things now."

"Before it's too late," Nathan agreed. Despite the double burdens of time and hard use, the old vehicle still held a gallant air. The Terraplane Pickup Express had been known from the beginning for its striking good looks. Both front and rear fenders were swept into long streamlined affairs. The front grill rose in what had once been known as a sunburst design, looking like something more at home on a racing sedan than a pickup. The front bumper was strongly veed, the doors were handcrafted steel and opened front-to-back.

Fuller moved up alongside him. "Sure is one impressive vehicle."

"One of the finest ever made," Nathan agreed. "An amazing design for its time, particularly since they launched it at the height of the Depression."

The mechanic joined the mayor in staring at him. "You know something about trucks, Doc?"

"A little." He pointed at the front assembly. "This was one of the first passenger vehicles ever to offer independent front suspension at no extra cost. Back then they called it Axle-Flex, and it made for a real improvement in the quality of ride. Individual seats with padded springs, another plus. Hudson also brought the instrument cluster in front of the driver. Most cars and virtually every other truck at that time had them over in the middle—easier to fit, but a lot harder for the driver to read."

The mayor and the mechanic exchanged glances. Fuller said quietly, "Is that a fact?"

But Nathan did not take notice. "The engine displaced two hundred and twelve cubic inches in an L-shaped six-cylinder configuration. They doubled the size of the oil pump and pinned the piston rings. The only other car to use such a concept then was Rolls Royce. That design, plus roller cam tappets and a new crankshaft with eight integrally-cast counterweights, allowed them to up the compression ratio to six to one. That baby could generate eighty-five horsepower. Quite a lot for its day."

Earl offered, "If this don't beat all, I don't know what does."

Fuller shook his head. "You're one for the surprises, Doc."

"I'll say." Earl stared at him with something akin to awe. "Surely do wish I knew what you'd just said."

Nathan focused on the two men. "Okay, this is what I want you to do. Start on a complete overhaul. Head to toe."

The two men gaped at him. Fuller said, "Come again?"

"I want you to take it apart right down to the frame, replace everything that's the least bit worn, even the bolts." Nathan felt as if he were organizing a surgical team. "I have some addresses of antique truck specialists. Call them, they'll find you what you need. But for starters, I want you to put in a completely rebuilt motor. Then do the shocks, electrical system, brakes, seat covers, the works."

Fuller's gaze swiveled from the truck to the doctor and back again. "Do you have any idea how much that's gonna cost?"

Nathan could not help grinning. "No, but I'm sure you'll tell me."

"Doc," the mechanic shook his head. "I gotta tell you, it'd be a darn sight cheaper just to buy a new truck for the gal."

"But it wouldn't be *this* truck. It wouldn't be Poppa Joe's." He stared at the battered rusty heap. "Any idea what color it was?"

"I seem to recollect it being blue." Earl's eyes were gradually igniting from the thought of what lay ahead. "Yeah, that's right. Had some kinda fancy name, but it was a deep sky blue."

"Match it as best you can, all right? And send the bumpers and grillwork off to be regalvanized." Nathan noticed the mayor did not share the mechanic's enthusiasm. "Don't worry, Fuller. I'll pay whatever it costs."

"I'm not worried about that." Fuller shook his head once more. "You sure got a way of shaming a man."

"What are you talking about?"

"All this for a woman who's done rained fire and brimstone down on you since you got here." The mayor was eyeing him curiously. "You sure got a funny way of paying back your enemies."

"Connie's not an enemy. She's a fine woman."

"Sure she is. But I never thought I'd hear you saying them words." Fuller reached over and gripped his arm. "Don't worry about the cost. I think there's gonna be others who'll want to jump on this idea."

"With both feet," Earl agreed, reaching for his toolbox. "You wait until word gets 'round about this one."

"I don't want word to get out," Nathan protested. "I want Connie to be surprised."

"Oh, she'll be surprised all right." Earl's head disappeared under the hood. "Shocked right outta her socks, I warrant."

"Come on, Doc. Let's leave the man to get started."

"The name is Nathan."

The mayor turned him around and guided him back outside. "Got to hand it to you, Nathan. This is gonna set the hens to clucking." Fuller's smile was broader than ever. "You done good, son. Real good."

Twenty-Two

The restaurant sat at the crest of a rise, so that it overlooked the Hillsboro valley on one side and Jonestown on the other. From their aerie perched high above the night-clad valleys, the towns looked like oddly matched twins. Yet only Jonestown was connected to the outside world by the thin concrete ribbon of a state highway. It was by far the larger of the two, a burgeoning little city with the clean rectangular shapes of new industry.

Connie followed Nathan's gaze through the tall windows that wrapped the entire way around their hilltop haven. "There but for the sake of a highway goes Hillsboro."

"The town looks, well, successful."

"It is. We're watching them saunter into a future that ought to be ours."

"Hillsboro is a nice place, Connie."

"Maybe so. But nice don't buy much in the way of groceries." Yet there was a new softness to her gaze, and to her tone. "I can't thank you enough for inviting me up here tonight. I've spent all day thinking about how much I needed to get away."

"Me too." He refrained from saying how it had taken him a half-hour to choose a tie. "I can't remember the last time I went out to something that wasn't related to work."

"Yes, so I've heard." The gaze deepened, the sorrow was shared. "I want to tell you again just how sorry I am about, well, everything."

Nathan started to respond with another apology of his own, but this time it was not enough. He sat up nearer the clouds than the towns and their earthly problems. Tonight was a time for opening up, for speaking without barriers. "For a while, the only defense I had against everything inside my head was rage."

"I understand."

It almost shocked him into stopping, how much empathy there was in her words and her eyes. But he had started, and now he wanted to finish. "The doctors at the clinic where I was treated after my breakdown, they said it was a natural part of the healing process. They said it would pass with time. I didn't believe them. I couldn't see how I could get out of something that had me so trapped."

She watched him with eyes that drank in his words. "What trapped you, Nathan?"

"Looking back, I don't know where one started and the other ended. The rage was so much a part of my battle against the enemy. That's what I called it, you know. Cancer. The enemy. I suppose that sounds, well, crazy."

"I don't think it's crazy at all. And not just because of Poppa Joe." She took a breath then, and gave him the best smile she could manage. "There, I said his name and didn't burst into tears."

"Do you want to talk about something else?"

"No. We'd just spend the night thinking about it. No. What I wanted to say was, I can't get over my visit to the hospital where you used to work. When I walked into the children's ward and saw those young kids lying there, I never knew I could hate anything as much as I did what was causing all those families pain."

Nathan gave a slow nod. "The other doctors, they were able to put it aside. I watched them, Connie. I know it's true, what I'm saying. They would leave the building and shrug off everything that was inside like they were taking off a lab coat." He marveled anew at their ability. "I knew they were right when they said I needed to do it. But I couldn't. I tried. But the work and all those suffering little kids, they trapped me. I carried them and their parents with me everywhere."

"You poor man." She reached across the table and took his hand. Her fingers were solid and warm and real. "You cared too much."

There in the restaurant, there with this woman, Nathan felt the old burning rise up once more. He felt the pain in his heart sear its way upward, and yet this time there was a rightness. He swallowed hard, and said, "They were such good kids, Connie. They deserved so much more than I could give them. They deserved a *life*."

She did not respond, except to release his hand and sit back and give him the space to collect himself.

He inspected the darkening vista for a time, then turned to look out over the restaurant. The walls were huge panes of glass supported by broad stone sheaths. The wall opposite the kitchen contained an inglenook fireplace with a hand-beaten copper flange. The ceiling was high and supported by a dozen beams the length and breadth of large trees.

When Nathan finally turned back to her and started to grimace an apology, she cut him off by saying, "My folks were killed when I was sixteen. I suppose you've heard that around town. It was one of those senseless things, a logging truck took a turn too wide, clipped their car, and sent them off the ledge. One minute alive and the greatest parents anybody ever had. The next and . . ."

It was her turn to look out over the valley. Then, "I think I've been living from my own fair-sized rage ever since. Only now, when I need it most, I seem to have lost the ability."

"I know what you mean," he said. "Somehow it feels like Poppa Joe's taken the rage from me." When Connie kept her gaze on the window and did not respond, he gave into the pressure of the thought welling up from inside. "I don't know if I can put this into words, but the whole time I was up there with him on the mountain, I felt like I was surrounded by a mystery. Everywhere I looked, I was seeing something I couldn't put into words. Something I wasn't actually seeing at all." He stopped, shrugged helplessly. "That sounds silly, doesn't it?"

"I don't think it sounds silly at all." She resumed her canted inspection of him. "He told me about how he was hoping you could help give him something to grant his passage meaning."

"Another mystery, another challenge. He is one amazing old man."

"You've got some amazements of your own." Connie managed a small smile. "Letting an old man's ruminations bother you so."

"I feel like he's settled this responsibility on my shoulders," Nathan confessed.

"And you're not minding?"

"No." Definite about that. "To be honest, I like it. Doesn't make it any easier to do, but the challenge itself feels, well, good."

"It draws you close to him," Connie murmured.

"Yes, it does." Darkness had swallowed the hillside and the clouds and the surrounding mountains, until now all he could see was the beckoning earthbound stars, and a ribbon of light where the highway traffic continued to stream. He saw Connie check her watch and took it as a signal to say, "I suppose we'd better be going."

The drive down was quiet and comforting. He took the curves easy, both because he did not know the road and because he was in no hurry to have the evening end. Finally he pulled into Connie's drive, cut the motor, and sat listening to the quiet winter night.

He said, "This has been great." Then he wished he had not spoken at all, for the words were so inadequate for what he felt.

Connie stirred in the seat beside him. "I was just thinking about something Hattie said to me a while ago. It was back when I used to baby-sit Dawn. One night Hattie and Chad came in from an evening do somewhere, and she told me it had done them a world of good to just get away and talk."

Nathan could only see her silhouette, a strong jaw, and an occasional glint of light catching her eyes. Eyes that held so much intelligence and life and down-to-earth common sense. He heard the sadness in her voice and started to reach out and touch her shoulder, but hesitated, not sure if she wanted it, not sure if she were still aware of where she was and who she was with.

"I asked Hattie, how could she need time to talk, she and Chad were in that store together sixteen hours a day. Hattie told me this was different. When they got away like that, it felt as though for those few hours everything was right with the world. Their problems weren't just a thousand miles away, they belonged to somebody else entirely." Connie turned to him then, and said softly, "I never understood what she was talking about. Until right now."

Twenty-Three

On Monday morning, three days before Christmas, Connie pushed through the loveliest two doors in all of Pritchard County. The rosewood frames had been carved by old Mr. Langdon himself, Duke's grandfather. Art deco vines crept around the central lead panes, with hand-sized lilies sprouting in profusion. Overhead yet another carving, this one curved in a half-moon shape, framed the old gilt letters declaring this to be Langdon's Emporium. Poppa Joe and many of the other old timers still called this the Emporium, and remembered when it was the finest place for shopping this side of Charlottesville.

The store's marble-clad interior rang with the sound of Christmas. It was more bright joy than she had heard that season, almost more than she could bear. Connie walked straight up to the first shop assistant. She vaguely recognized the young lady from church, so she dredged up a semblance of a smile before demanding, "Is Duke around?"

"He's here somewhere, Miss Wilkes. I saw him earlier." Her smile was as bright as her yellow chiffon dress. "Let me call upstairs."

"Miss Connie?" Duke's voice spun her about. He walked over with a worried frown. "Something the matter with Poppa Joe?"

"Nothing more than usual." She fought against the bloom of pain which his concern brought to her chest. Which was passing strange. People all over town asked about little else. "Can we talk?"

"Oh. Yes, ma'am, I suppose we can." All the air left that big frame, spaced with the words. Duke led her toward the back. "It's about Dawn and me, isn't it."

"Yes." She knew her voice was clipped, and she found herself wishing for an instant that the familiar old anger was still there to draw on. But its absence had become a part of nursing Poppa Joe, as though the love she tried to show the old man dispelled her ability to fight against the world. And she would allow nothing to come between herself and his own last few days.

Which meant that when Duke ushered her through the back double doors and into the quiet coffee alcove for the store's employees, she felt as deflated as he looked. "Duke, what on earth am I going to do with you?"

"Miss Connie, I wish there was something I could say that would make it all right. I done everything I know how. I practiced all sorts of speeches, I prayed myself silly. I talked to the pastor, I talked to Hattie and Chad, I talked with Dawn until we're both sick of talking. I even talked with Poppa Joe."

"What did he say?"

Duke turned shameful. "I wish you wouldn't ask me that, Miss Connie."

"But I am." Connie allowed herself to be settled into a chair by the corner table. "What did Poppa Joe tell you, Duke?"

The young man lowered himself into a chair opposite her and sighed another set of words. "He said you did just fine, for a lady who insisted on walking forwards while looking backwards."

The insight cut like a knife, so much that she drew back. Duke looked at her, frightened now. "I didn't mean on telling you, Miss Connie. Please don't get any madder than you already are."

"I'm not mad," she said weakly.

"You're not?"

"Oh, Duke, I wish I could be. But I can't. Poppa Joe's robbed me of all my anger. He's left me nothing but my fears." She couldn't even draw up a tear, just a hollow sense of defeat and a voice that rang flat in her own ears. "Do you really think it's right for you to marry Dawn?"

His face took on such a fierce resolution she found her breath catching in her throat. "Yes, ma'am. I do. And so does Dawn."

"But she's so young."

There was a trace of Poppa Joe there, a sense of looking back through time to the younger uncle she still remembered in the darkness of her lonely nights. "I know that. But I tell you something, Miss Connie. In some ways she's already got more in that head and heart than most women twice her age."

Again Connie felt the commonsense strength pushing at her. When she did not respond, Duke went on. "I know what you see when you look at me. You see a country bumpkin. The only thing I ever did right in my life was choosing my folks."

"Duke—"

"Now hold on, Miss Connie. You done let me get started. I won't take long." Duke took a breath. "I'm not smart like you or Dawn. But I do know if I kept this store all to myself, I'd run it straight into the ground."

Before, she had seen him as a vacuum dressed up in a handsome form and a fine face and a shock of dark hair. But there was a keenness to his voice and his gaze that startled her. Here was one who held to hillfolk honesty, even when the sharpness of fair observation cut like a skinning knife.

Duke continued, "Dawn, now, she's got the smarts for both of us. And she loves me for what I am."

"What are you, Duke?" And she meant it. Connie no longer felt as though she knew. As though up to now she had only seen what she had feared—a threat to her tenuous position with Dawn.

"I'm a simple-hearted mountain boy. I love these hills and this valley and this town. I love the Lord, and I love my Dawn. I aim on doing right by all of them. All my life long." He sat up straight, and in that moment his shoulders looked broad enough to bear the burdens of this entire town. "But I need help. I need somebody who'll have the brains to teach me what I can learn, and help me through what I can't. Dawn's like that, Miss Connie."

"I know," she murmured, and swiped at the burning at the edges of her eyes. Why now? Why should she feel so defeated and crushed? How was it possible to try so hard to do what was right, and end up getting one thing after another so horribly wrong?

Duke leaned forward and planted his elbows on his knees. His eyes were fired with a direct force, undimmed by years or disguise. "Miss Connie, Dawn's gonna be my right hand here in Langdon's. My folks want to retire, and they been worried about what's gonna happen once I take over. Leastwise, they were. But we've spent a lot of nights talking, the four of us. They're settled in their thinking now. Dawn's showed 'em. She's as good with them as she is with everybody. They love her, Miss Connie. They've taken to calling Dawn the daughter they didn't ever have."

But what about me, Connie wanted to cry. *Who's going to be my little girl?* But she could not speak. There was nothing to be said. Nothing at all.

Connie forced herself to her feet. "I have to be going. Tell Dawn I'm happy for her. And for you."

"Miss Connie, please—"

But she could not take any more right then. She had to get away and think about it. She spoke, though the words felt like dust to her tongue. "Tell Dawn my Christmas gift to the both of you is my blessing."

Twenty-Four

The daily change in Poppa Joe grew ever sharper. When Nathan arrived on Christmas Eve he tried to keep his anxiety trapped inside, but both Connie and Hattie clearly noticed how Poppa Joe's decline rocked him. The old man was scarcely able to sit upright in the wheelchair. His face looked as if it belonged on a cadaver.

Connie greeted him with a voice twisted by worry. "You come in here and talk some sense to him."

Nathan stepped into the parlor and squatted down by the wheelchair. Poppa Joe looked at him with eyes both weak and determined. "They're having the evening service to mark our Savior's birth. I ain't missed it in fifty years. More."

Nathan started to speak, started to play the role he had been trained for. But something in that face stopped him. "You really want to put yourself through this?"

Up close the doddering was constant, the stress caused by keeping his head upright painfully evident. Poppa Joe murmured, "Help me, son. Please."

"How are you feeling?"

"Distressed," came the rasping reply. Even this close to the end, the eyes probed with focused passion. "Sorely distressed. Wish I knew what I'm gonna take to set before my Lord."

He patted the old man's arm, the movement in time to the carillon toll of his own heart. In that instant he realized the plea for assistance was not just over going to church that night. Nathan could see the ticking of the clock, the draining away of any opportunity to respond to the old man's challenge, there upon his ravaged features. "You don't want an injection now, I take it."

A fraction of a headshake. "Only put me to sleep. Maybe the Lord'll speak to me in His house. Got to be awake to hear."

Nathan swiveled around to where Connie and Hattie stood with shoulders touching, taking comfort from each other's closeness. He watched Connie wring her hands, striving to hold to her composure, seeing how she wanted to yell and order and push her weight about. Yet he sensed she was held by the same force that was directing him.

Nathan asked, "Who do we know that has a truck and won't have left for church yet?"

The question caught them both off guard. Hattie recovered first and glanced at the clock on the mantel. "Duke Langdon was coming by our place to pick up Dawn in about five minutes."

"That's the young man I met up at Poppa Joe's cabin, isn't it?" Nathan rose to his feet, pleased he would have a strong man to help out. "Go call and ask them to meet me at the clinic."

Connie started, "But he's . . ."

Nathan crossed the room, placed his hands on her upper arms, and tried to pour out his own strength and concern with his gaze. "I know," he said softly. "But Poppa Joe wants this, Connie. He *needs* this."

Then he waited. It was her decision. If she objected, he would allow the professional side of his nature to take control, and together they would settle the old man where he should have been all along, back in bed. But if she didn't, well, then he knew what his heart was calling him to do. Despite all the logic in the world, he knew.

Evidently so did Connie. She gave a tiny nod and whispered, "All right."

"Good." He turned away, both from her and from the arguments racing through his own mind. "I'll be back from the clinic just as fast as I can."

Even before the dust settled in the clinic's driveway, the truck's bright red doors opened and out tumbled two of the finest looking young people Nathan had ever seen. He could not help but compare their fresh strength with the old man's weakness as they came running over. Nor could he help but see how their features mirrored those of Connie and Hattie, the pinched compression binding them all together more tightly than words ever could.

Dawn said, "Momma told us Poppa Joe's going fast."

"She's right." There was no place for empty words or false hopes. "You both need to be strong now. For Poppa Joe and for Connie."

Duke clenched his jaw so tight it looked like he held a walnut in each cheek. He reached over and took hold of Dawn's hand. When he was certain she had recovered her composure, he looked up and said, "Tell us what we need to do."

Nathan pointed to the mattress and the stretcher and the IV unit at his feet. "We need to load these in the truck." As Duke started forward, Nathan added, "Dawn, go call the church and tell them to expect us."

The preparations made, they swiftly covered the distance back to Connie's house. With a minimum of words they took the old man out of the wheelchair and settled him into the stretcher. Two quilts were laid under him to pad Poppa Joe's protruding bones. Another was settled on top and tucked in around the edges. A second pillow was added. Nathan carried the IV unit and the tubing in his bag, along with two filled syringes. Whatever else, Poppa Joe would not suffer during what would most likely be his final outing.

The four of them knelt around the stretcher, waiting for

a reaction from the old man. He looked up at them, eyes bright and clear now that the stress was gone and the thing he wanted was growing closer. He nodded once, and said in the whisper that had become his voice, "I'm much obliged."

Nathan said, "I know you won't take a shot now, it'd only put you to sleep. But if the pain starts getting bad, all you need to do look my way. I've got everything ready."

He rose to his feet, dusted his trousers, and nodded to Duke. With Nathan at the feet and Duke taking the head, they raised the stretcher and carried it outside. Duke proved his agility by not tilting the stretcher one iota, even as he slid into the truck and pulled Poppa Joe in after him. They settled Poppa Joe and the stretcher onto the mattress, then Nathan and Connie seated themselves on the opposite rails.

The evening air was bitingly brisk, the sky turned a ruddy gold by trails of lingering dusk. Nathan watched the trees and the sunset play across the old man's face. Poppa Joe's eyes were bright and wide-open, drinking in all he was able to see. Especially the sky.

Word had clearly gotten out, for the yard in front of the church was packed to overflowing. The crowd grew so quiet a baby's whimper seemed out of place, as together Duke and Nathan lifted the stretcher and carried it from the truck.

Then the murmurs washed over them all. People stood in the manner of country folk, the women with hands crossed at the middle, the men with hands in their pockets or fiddling with the brims of their hats.

Their passage toward the church was slow but steady. People reached out to touch the stretcher or Nathan's arm, murmuring words of welcome. He felt as though the greeting kindled a flame in the center of his chest.

Will Green was there by the door, nodding his welcome with the others. Then Will said to Nathan and Connie both, "Me and the boys, we were wondering if maybe we could come by and play some of the old favorites for Poppa Joe."

Connie responded, "I didn't know you still made music, Will."

"Don't hardly play for nobody but the fellers and the dogs these days." The old hat did a steady nervous revolution between his fingers. "But we got to talking last night, and were just wondering if maybe we could stop by this weekend with the instruments. Be our way of giving this season a proper meaning, if you see what I'm after."

Connie glanced down at her uncle, who responded with a single nod. She said to Will, "Sunset is his best time."

"We'll be there Saturday, Miss Connie. Poppa Joe." He turned to Nathan and nodded. "Good to see you here, Doc."

Inside the church they met yet another crowd, all of them on their feet to give quiet homage to a fine old man.

The front pew had been saved for them. They settled the stretcher there in front of the altar, and waited as Reverend Brian Blackstone and his wife came over to welcome Poppa Joe. The old man had trouble guiding his hand into that of the pastor's. That was the only moment when the women lost control.

Even as the choir led them through a rousing series of Christmas hymns, the church remained caught by a more somber tone. Nathan sang along with the others, and knew he shared with them the mood and the moment. From time to time he glanced about the church, wondering at the seeming lack of disharmony. This was Christmas Eve, yet the people did not seem reluctant to show a melancholy side. In their faces he found the same stolid acceptance they showed in facing their illnesses. As though here and now, when life struck in ways that others might call unfair, they showed the strength which was truly all their own.

Nathan heard little of what the pastor had to say, at least at first. His attention was held by the old man lying there before him. Poppa Joe kept his eyes fastened upon Reverend Blackstone with a force that belied his body's weakness. He did not hear the words, he *consumed* them. He listened with a hunger so fierce there was scarcely strength left for him to draw breath.

Nathan found his heart pulled out of shape by conflicting desires—part of him wanting to retain the shattered fragments of all he once had been, yet another part hungering for what he scarcely could identify. There was more to this than simply giving Poppa Joe something to carry to heaven—he was not even sure he understood what the old man meant by that. Rather, he sought something *worthy*—something which would help give form to all the transformations he was discovering inside himself, all the mysteries taking shape.

He was pondering hard on this when the pastor's words shot into focus. One moment it was a calming background drone, a cadence almost in keeping with his own thoughts. The next, and the pastor glanced Nathan's way. Their eyes locked, and Nathan felt a shiver run through him. There was a sense of sharing something beyond the realm of words. And in that moment Nathan knew that now was the time. He *knew*.

"Many of the lessons God wishes for us to learn," Reverend Blackstone then said, "are based on the principle of *release*. We need to learn how to take our hands off the controls. When we are at our most desperate, and our desire to cling to control is strongest, this is when we most need to let go. To be willing in faith to take our hands off, and put the experience and the circumstances under the control of God."

Nathan's sense of knowing did not arrive in an explosive flash. The mystery was too great to be touched with power. Otherwise he would probably have been blinded. It came with the natural growth of a seedling which pressed up through the dark earth to finally find the light.

Reverend Blackstone continued, "Yet we desperately want to direct our own lives. It is fear which keeps us from releasing control. It makes us skeptical. It keeps us from believing in the goodness of God. Friends, a moment given over to fear is a moment lost from God. We are lost in that moment, trapped by fear and doubt and a desperate desire to cling to what we know."

Nathan looked down at Poppa Joe and studied the old man's clear gaze. Untainted by age or hardship or loss or illness or pain. Even as the light now dimmed, still the power was there. And for the first time in his life, Nathan understood that the reason was because the power was not his own.

"And yet at these times we can do ourselves the greatest harm by trying to forge ahead alone, governed by fear, blinded by our terrors and our pains and our past. It is at this moment when release of control to God is vital. This is no senseless casting everything to the winds of fate. This is *trusting God.* This is putting action to the theory of faith."

Nathan knew. It was time. All the changes and all the mysteries which had swirled like tendrils of invisible fog through the days and nights since his arrival, all snapped into a focus so strong he knew the vision was not his own. It was time. He had been shown the door, he was invited to enter. His friends had gathered to help him, the old man had asked in the kindest way anyone ever would. There would never be a moment less trammeled with doubts and hesitations. It no longer mattered that he did not understand everything, or that so many of his questions remained unanswered. The comfort and peace and power he felt were more real than anything else his entire life had contained. It was time.

"Remember when the Israelites were trapped between the forces of Pharaoh and the impossible sea? Moses turns to them and in Exodus fourteen, verse thirteen, he says, 'Do not be afraid. *Stand still*, and see the salvation of the Lord, which He will accomplish for you today.'"

Nathan's heart hammered in his chest. His hands grew so clammy, he wiped them continually down the sides of his trouser legs. Connie cast him an odd look, but he remained caught by what was about to come. He had not been this frightened since his final exams in medical school. Frightened, and yet excited. Excited, and yet incredibly calm. It was amazing how he could be all of these things at once.

"In our impossible times, when our human frailties are greatest, that is when God's power can be strongest. If only we can release the impossibilities to God, He will work His miracles. Free yourself from the deadly assumption that you have the strength and the wisdom and the capacity to make the right decisions yourself. That you can find your way through this alone. Give it up. Turn it over. And then, once you have given it over, *leave* the circumstances and the problems in God's hands. Release control to God, and step off the cliff of comfort into the unknown."

For the first time since beginning the sermon, Pastor Blackstone looked down at Poppa Joe. His eyes lingered there on the man, a sad smile creasing his features. "Some of you might be wondering why I chose to speak about fear on a night of rejoicing over our Savior's birth."

The pastor held Poppa Joe's gaze a moment longer, then seemed to gather himself with a great breath that drew him up to twice his normal size. "I do so because we celebrate here tonight the *conquest of fear*. Friends, I stand here tonight to proclaim the good news to all the world. Fear is vanquished! Death is conquered! Tonight we celebrate not only the Savior's birth, but His death. Why? Because the Lord was made flesh with one purpose in mind—to come so that He might die for us and for our sins. Because through Christ's death a door was opened. An eternal invitation was made. To all who suffer and worry and hurt and know fear, our Savior says, 'Come! Come and I will give you rest! Come and drink the cup of eternal healing! Come and sing at the holy feast of life! Come and celebrate! Why? Because I, your King, have conquered death. I, your King, have conquered fear.' The door is open, our way made straight. The King reigns in the eternal Kingdom, and we are His people! Hallelujah, Amen!"

When the sermon ended and the final song began, Nathan stepped into the aisle. He walked forward and met the pastor's outstretched hand, said words he could scarcely get around his oversized heart, and nodded when the pastor asked if he was sure he wanted to bring Christ into his life.

Nathan knelt there with the pastor at the edge of the podium, feeling the hand on his head and listening to the words spoken over him. He heard the music and the voices welling up around him. And he found himself reaching out, joining with the town and the valley and the Spirit which dwelled there in those hills. Binding him together with love.

When Nathan returned to his seat he found himself unable to meet anyone's eye. Except, that is, for Poppa Joe.

The old man signaled with another feeble movement. Nathan bent over the stretcher, glad for a reason to lower himself from the stares of the congregation. The organ and the music and the hymn almost took away the weakened words. Almost, but not quite.

Poppa Joe murmured to him, "I'm ready now. I done found the answer I've been looking for."

Twenty-Five

Christmas Day was a subdued affair. Nathan allowed the morning visit with Poppa Joe to stretch into an early lunch with Connie and the Campbells. No one tried for a false sense of Christmas spirit, which was good. No one mentioned the previous evening's events at the altar, which was better. Nathan did not regret his actions. Not at all. But he was by nature a very private man, and such a huge change required a period of settling in. Somehow these new friends of his seemed to understand. Not even Poppa Joe felt a need to mention it, except for one time. As Nathan helped him settle into the wheelchair so that he could eat lunch with the others, Poppa Joe gave him a look that pierced straight to his heart, and simply said, "I'm much obliged, son. Much obliged."

The remainder of the week strung out hard and long. Nathan seemed to spend all of Friday and much of Saturday running from one emergency to another. So it was that he did not arrive at Connie's until just before sunset that Saturday evening. And was surprised to find it necessary to park half a block away.

The day held to a coolness more in keeping with spring than winter. Even with the sun creasing the western hills and sending farewell streamers out over the sky, still he was comfortable walking down the street in shirtsleeves. Connie's driveway and the spaces directly in front of her house were packed with five pickups and seven cars and a cluster of easy-standing hillfolk. The women had a hard-scrubbed look, their print dresses and fancy aprons washed until the colors had faded. The men were in starched coveralls or the bottom half of dark suits and their best white shirts buttoned up to their collars. Nathan counted two dozen visitors in all, plus about as many dogs. The animals sauntered around or sat in the back of the trucks or stood by their masters, showing the easy companionship of well-trained hunters.

Nathan walked over, greeted the assembly, and was welcomed in turn by a smile from Connie. The expression tugged at his heart. The gathering seemed to have drawn her out from beneath her covering of fatigue and worry.

Whatever else these people were here for, Nathan decided, it was for the good of all concerned.

"Hey there, Doc." Will Green stepped from the circle and offered a hard slab of a hand. "How you keeping?"

"Fine." Nathan continued to be surprised how these country people managed to match hands like granite with grips as soft as feathers. Will's hand barely squeezed, just took his own, held it a moment, then let it go. "All these people are in your band?"

That brought a chorus of smiles from the gathering. "Shoot, Doc, we don't have nothing so fancy as a band."

"We heard Will here was gonna come over and play for Poppa Joe," a pinched-faced woman said quietly. "We asked if we could come too."

"We's all friends of Poppa Joe's," another voice said.

"And kin from way back," Connie added.

"Shucks, Miss Connie, ain't hardly nobody in this valley who's not kin, you go back far enough."

"You're all welcome," Connie said. "But Poppa Joe's been coming and going all afternoon. He's here one minute, and asleep the next."

"Don't matter none," Will offered. "We'll just fill in the spaces best we can."

"When he woke up earlier I reminded him you were coming to play," Connie went on. "He said to tell you it'd be nice to have you bring the mountains down close to where he could touch them one more time."

That brought a pause to the group. One of the women raised her starched apron and wiped at one corner of her eye. Will heaved a sigh and said, "Guess we might as well set up."

They waited until the instruments were unlimbered and tuned before disturbing Poppa Joe. Hattie and Dawn had arrived by then, there to keep Connie company through the slow hours of another lingering dusk. Together with Nathan they lifted the old man, under-quilt and all, and settled him back on the stretcher. Poppa Joe was far too weak to use his wheelchair. With Connie and Dawn at the feet and Nathan taking the head, they walked him out to the porch.

Poppa Joe was wide-eyed and silent as he took in the people. There were four mandolins, three fiddles, two banjos, a bass fiddle, a washboard, four tambourines, and six guitars. Two men who clearly had no interest in either playing or singing rose from their seats on the front steps to greet Poppa Joe. Those there to sing and not play formed a little semicircle beyond the trellis.

They settled him at the corner of the porch where he could see both the players and the singers. Once he was down and those who had carried him had found comfortable spots around the stretcher, a silence gathered. No one seemed able to speak. The day's warmth continued to linger, even as the sun stroked the western peaks.

The assembly waited, their gazes fixed upon the old man. Their emotions were a palpable force. Then a bird sang a single note, clear as the sky. A sound of crystal promise, a swift chime of hope.

A voice as soft as a breeze through the last of autumn's leaves whispered from the stretcher, "Evening, all."

The group smiled as best they could, and breathed easier. Will asked, "You got any favorites, Poppa Joe?"

"I like 'em all," he murmured, and waved a feeble hand.

"Well, then," Will said, "Let's start with them what everybody knows." He hefted his fiddle, and swung into "She'll Be Coming 'Round the Mountain." The beginning was a little scratchy, as people found their places and their voices and began concentrating upon the music and not what had brought them there.

The second song got them moving, and the third had the chorus doing soft little hand claps, alternating one hand on top of the other.

By the fourth, doors were opening up and down the street, and people were walking over. While a few joined the choir, the others seemed content to stand along the edge of the street and smile and nod and weave in time to the music.

The musicians ran through a host of old favorites—"Just As I Am," "When The Saints," "Swing Low, Sweet Chariot," "I Saw The Light," "Amazing Grace," "I've Got A Feeling," "This Train." The longer they played, the happier and larger grew the crowd, the stronger the voices, the more commanding the rhythm. Smiles blossomed like flowers on an early spring field.

Poppa Joe stayed with them most of the time. His eyes touched face after face. The smiles which greeted him were so sad Nathan could not watch for long. So much emotion within these quiet simple people. So much caring. Such a noble way to say farewell to one of their own.

When they started on a rousing chorus of "The Tennessee Waltz," the old man was smiling and Connie was rocking from side to side. Nathan rose from his seat, at first planning to get the two ladies some cushions to soften their places on the porch planking. But he caught sight of young children spinning and giggling in the lawn. Then he saw Connie's eyes opened wide, half in fear and half in hope. And it was the most natural thing in the world to reach out his hand for hers.

There were a few good-natured chuckles. But not many. Neighbors and musicians watched and smiled as Nathan waltzed around the open space at the center of the porch. It was not like him to be the focus of attention. But just now, in the dimming light of a lovely Shenandoah winter's dusk, he did not care. Connie blushed her way through the dance, meeting his eyes only once. But that look was all the reward he needed.

When they stopped, a quintet of smiles welcomed them back to their places by the stretcher. Hattie and Chad and Duke and Dawn all mirrored Poppa Joe's quiet satisfaction, their approval given equally to them both.

The old man's eyes began to droop, yet he did not ask for his injection. Nathan kept a careful watch, but felt there was no need to press. Poppa Joe would ask when he was ready. Every once in a while, the gaze would strengthen, and he would look first at his niece, and then at Nathan. He found himself waiting for those glances, drinking in all that was unsaid. All the mysteries.

Hattie drew Dawn inside. A few minutes later they came back with candles and set them around the porch. Someone joined the assembly with a pair of Coleman lanterns. Their glow added to the dusk's fading gold, backlighting all the people gathered around the house.

There came a sense of a natural pause. Poppa Joe's eyes finally closed, his breathing eased. Connie went inside and came back with another quilt which she settled around her uncle's form. Nathan sighed from the fullness and the sadness, and found he could see his breath, which was a surprise, because he had not noticed the growing chill at all.

Will Green signaled to the choir by lifting his fiddle, and he alone started into a song which seemed to drift from Nathan's most distant memories. The women joined in naturally, their voices as soft as the sunset's last rosy hues. "I will arise and go to Jesus," they sang, and all the gathering seemed to catch and hold their breath.

Nathan found himself captured by the words and the moment, though his eyes remained held by Poppa Joe. A new force entered with the softness of the voices, a power so potent it squeezed his very soul. A tear escaped, pressed out by whatever it was that gathered there with the people and the night. He let it go, unhindered and unashamed. He watched the old man's breath grow softer and softer, and heard the ladies sing, "In the arms of my dear Savior, O there are ten thousand charms."

The last sound lingered, the bow scratched its way across the strings, and then the force was too great. No one else could move, or sing, or do anything but stand there and wait. Wait as the old man stilled, and the force pressed them all into one unified whole, burning with the power of a love far beyond this world and this fragile thing called life. Wait and feel the Spirit leave, and take the old man away.

Connie knelt there beside him for a long moment, then finally managed to whisper through her tears, "Poppa Joe has gone Home."

Twenty-Six

There were far fewer tears at the funeral than Connie would have expected. Even from herself.

The church service seemed to come and go in an instant, which surprised her as well. Normally funerals seemed to drag on forever. But long before she was ready, she was walking out of the church and into the bitter cold day. The sky was no sky at all, just a covering of finest gauze, a shroud so thin the sun could still be seen, a brilliant guest to this strange and unmournful day.

She walked with a dry-eyed Hattie and Dawn from the church. Nathan walked behind them, alongside Chad Campbell and Duke Langdon, because she had asked him to. She had worked up the nerve to ask Nathan because she had been afraid she was going to lose control, and she did not want to be left to cling to someone else's man. Now she was glad she had done it, simply because his closeness was nice. Strange that anything could be called that on such a day, but it was the truth.

Six of the musicians carried the coffin, led by a somber Will Green. It was her way of thanking the men who had made that final night sing and had brought the mountains down for Poppa Joe to touch one last time.

Chad and Nathan sat up front as Duke drove his father's huge dark Lincoln behind the hearse. Connie was seated directly behind Nathan, and spent the time looking out the window at the town and the hills. Finally Hattie reached over and gripped her hand. "How are you feeling, dear?"

"Like I've been waiting all morning for the sadness and the keening to begin." Connie turned from her window, and had to smile at the astonishment on the two women's faces. "You want to know how I feel? Fine. Does that sound crazy?"

Dawn answered before her mother. "I don't think it sounds crazy at all. I'm sitting here feeling sad on one side and good on the other."

Hattie confessed, "I keep thinking about that send-off Will and the boys gave Poppa Joe."

"Me too." Dawn touched Duke's shoulder. "You think maybe you could arrange something like that for me when my time comes, honey?"

Duke shook his head. "I don't like this kind of wild talk at all."

Chad smiled at him. "Better get used to it, son, if you're going to marry into this family."

Connie looked from one face to the other, saw the humor there with the sadness. She turned to the one person still staring straight ahead. "What about you, Nathan?"

He stirred but did not turn around. "I was thinking about . . . before."

All of the car's passengers knew enough of that story to sober up. But Nathan took no notice. He kept staring forward and said thoughtfully, "I never went to a funeral. Not once. I couldn't stand the thought of going. It was like bowing down in public to my own defeat."

Connie felt her heart reach out with her hand as she leaned forward and grasped his shoulder. Nathan turned his head slightly at the touch, but not so far as to show her his eyes. Instead he reached up and took hold of her hand with his own. The touch was warm, and soft in the way of a strong man who knows how to be gentle. Out of the corner of her eye Connie saw Hattie give Dawn a look, but she kept her hand where it was.

Nathan went on, "But this doesn't seem at all like I had expected. I don't feel like there's a defeat here. Not in the slightest."

The car was quiet for a time, until Connie asked for them all, "What does it feel like?"

Nathan was silent until they reached the cemetery's gates. As they drove between the ivy-covered pillars, he said quietly, "It feels like a healing."

At the gravesite Connie sat down because it was expected of her. Reverend Brian Blackstone did a wonderful job of laying his old friend to rest. The town had turned out almost to a man, and they stood there in somber calm paying their final respects. Connie felt surprisingly good about it all, despite the hollow space that up to now had been filled by her uncle's presence. Dawn and Hattie and Chad sat there beside her, with Nathan and Duke standing behind them. Surrounded by friends and people she had known her life long. And they in turn were surrounded by their beloved hills. And God was in it all. She knew that without an instant's hesitation.

She missed her uncle, she missed her parents, life was far from perfect. Connie took a deep breath, filled by a remarkable combination of sadness and contentment. She was far from alone, and the life she had ahead of her held so much to look forward to. How on earth she could think of such things as they lowered Poppa Joe into the ground was beyond her comprehension. But she wanted to be honest with herself this day. This and every day to come. And to be perfectly honest, she was indeed too full to be anything but content.

Three Sundays later, Connie knocked and peeked around the open door. "Brian, do you have a minute?"

The pastor swiveled his chair around from where he had been staring out his back window. "Connie, hello, what a nice surprise, come in." He stood and walked around his desk. "I was busy daydreaming."

Her nerves betrayed themselves with the double grip she had on her purse. "I wanted to thank you for the service you did for Poppa Joe. I'm sorry it's taken so long to get by and tell you, but . . ."

"Don't give it another thought." He ushered her into a chair. "Would you like a cup of coffee?"

"I'm fine, thanks."

"You know, it's strange, but I'm still getting comments about that Christmas Eve service." He went back around and seated himself. "Seems a lot of people have been touched by Poppa Joe's passage. Attendance is up almost ten percent, did you know that?"

"No, no, I hadn't noticed."

"It's interesting you should stop by today, actually. I was planning to come see you later this week." His gaze drifted back toward the window, as though drawn by the memory which was bringing a little smile to his face. "I had quite a remarkable discussion this morning with another visitor."

But she did not want to hear about other visitors. Not now. It had taken three weeks of arguing with herself to get this far. "Brian, it's actually, well, there's something I need to talk with you about."

That caused him to put his smile away and bring her into full focus. "Of course, Connie. How are you getting on?"

"Fine. I'm fine. I'm, well . . ." The grip on her purse tightened. "One night I had a talk with Poppa Joe. He asked me, he said . . ."

Brian settled back, sort of drawing away, giving her room to breathe and step through this at her own pace. But not speaking. Not urging.

She took a breath and pushed it out in one quick rush.

"He said he was looking for a way to give a meaning to his passage. I've been thinking a lot about that. And I've been thinking about what you said on the road that day, when you said people like me were the hardest to reach. And that I needed to do more than just get by."

His smile was back, softer now. "It's nice to know you found my words worthy to remember."

"I think . . . you were right, Brian. I've been going through the motions for too long. I'm fine now, really. I mean, better than fine. It's not like I'm, you know, not coping or anything. But I want to live for more than just getting by day to day. Poppa Joe, he . . ." And then the breath was finished. Connie felt defeated by her own inability to voice what she was so unsure of.

"Poppa Joe lived for his hills and his Lord," Brian offered quietly. "He had the gift of a faith that moved with him, breathed with him, carried him through the good and the bad."

"Yes." Connie was so relieved to be understood, a wave of weakness flowed through her. "That's him."

"And in his talk, he left you with the feeling that maybe you needed to do more and be more."

"Like he was asking me to grow up," Connie agreed.

"That's a wonderful legacy to offer both his memory and your God," Brian said. He steepled his fingers. "Nathan Reynolds and I are going to start meeting Thursday nights for Bible study. Would you like to join us?"

She felt herself blushing suddenly. "Nathan?"

"He's a wonderful man, Connie." Brian's eyes illuminated the office's quiet shadows. "I'm so glad you're becoming friends with him."

"I . . . Yes." She felt as if the floor were shifting beneath her chair. "A Bible study would be nice."

"Sadie has a women's group she's trying to put together, an outreach program for the poorer families up the valley. Nathan's volunteered his time. We could certainly use some help with coordinating our efforts."

So many doors opening. Some seen, others still hidden from view. "Count me in."

"Good. I'm so very glad." The smile strengthened. "Now I have something else to talk with you about. We were wondering if maybe we could borrow Poppa Joe's meadow next Sunday."

"I suppose so." Connie cocked her head to one side. "Brian Blackstone, what are you not telling me?"

"It's a surprise, Connie. And it's not my surprise to be telling you about. Just promise me you'll be there next Sunday afternoon."

Twenty-Seven

As the week wore on, Connie found herself receiving little smirks and how-dos made musical by a secret she was not party to. Just walking down Main Street became an exercise in pretending she did not see what was making her quietly simmer. People crossed the street just to be able to smile their mystery in her face and to talk about anything under the sun except what she did not know.

By Thursday afternoon she had had enough. She stopped by Campbell's Grocery for a few items, and found Hattie and Dawn clustered at the checkout counter sharing a good giggle. Connie felt something snap inside. "I'll have you know it's not nice to laugh behind somebody's back. And it's ten times worse to do it to their face!"

"Why Connie, darling, we're not laughing at you." Hattie turned her grin toward her daughter. "Are we, Dawn, dear?"

"Hattie Campbell, if your grin was any bigger it'd show your back dentures."

"What a horrid thing to say. I don't wear dentures and you know it."

"Well, maybe we can correct that." Connie planted hands on her hips. "I want to know what's going on around this town, and I want to know right now!"

Dawn gave her innocent round eyes. "What, you mean about the church picnic?"

Connie stared at her. "A picnic? In January?"

Hattie said, "You don't have to be warm to eat."

Dawn added, "Up at Poppa Joe's meadow. Didn't anybody tell you?"

She looked from one woman to the other, felt her gaze narrow at the sight of half-hidden smiles. "You're not telling me the truth, not the one, nor the other."

"Why Connie Wilkes, what a thing to say." Dawn raised her hand. "May my dear sweet momma wash my mouth out with lye soap and carbolic acid if I'm talking fibs."

"What a positively horrid thought." Hattie's eyes crinkled at the edges toward Connie. "I just don't know what to do with this child any more."

"She's too much like her mother for her own good." Connie worked to hold on to her ire. "If all that's going on is a picnic, why wouldn't Brian tell me about it himself?"

"Maybe because Miss Nosy Britches is supposed to be the guest of honor," Dawn said, tossing her blonde hair. "And ought to be willing to show a little patience."

"Patience is a worthy virtue," Hattie agreed solemnly. "Especially for a woman of your age."

"You know perfectly well you're nine months older than

me, Hattie Campbell," Connie kept her eyes on Dawn. "Why on earth would anybody want to make me guest of honor at a picnic?"

"That's exactly what we were just talking about, isn't it, Momma?"

Connie stared at them, defeated by their good humor. She picked up her groceries and snapped over her shoulder, "You two are about half as sharp as you think you are."

"One o'clock Sunday afternoon, Connie dear," Hattie called. "Chad and I will drive by to pick you up."

That evening, the sight of Chad's car and Duke Langdon's truck both parked in the pastor's drive was almost enough to turn Connie around. But when she thought of who else was supposed to be there, Connie felt a warmth flood her face and neck.

There was none of the afternoon's bantering when she entered. Hattie and Dawn were friendly but subdued, saying simply they thought a weekly Bible study was long overdue. Chad looked as content as ever. Duke was wary and warm in turns, depending on whether his attention was on Connie or Dawn.

The evening passed too quickly. Brian was a delightful teacher, sketching their first passage in Romans, drawing them out with questions that invited them to think, to delve.

Connie found herself casting swift little glances toward Nathan, observing things anew. How his knife-edged features seemed softened by the light in his eyes. How his dark hair had tiny threads of silver-gray. How he listened to Brian with the same intensity he showed in the clinic, a total involvement with the matter at hand.

Toward the end of the evening, Connie felt as though the night caught its breath. It startled her, for the sensation was identical to the night of her talk with Poppa Joe. She looked around, wondering if anyone else felt the same. But they were nodding and listening and reading, continuing as though the night were just the same. But it wasn't. Something was very different. A sense of soft and gentle power grew around her, a drawing in so intense that nothing outside this room and this moment had any importance whatsoever. She looked at them, her oldest friend and her first love and their daughter and Dawn's fiancé. She studied the town's doctor, the pastor and his wife whom she had known since childhood, and felt as though she were seeing them for the first time. A faint light seemed to surround them, an illumination she felt with her heart. She took a shaky breath. Strange how the night had somehow taken on a holy cast.

"Connie?"

She turned and realized they were watching her. Brian asked, "Are you all right?"

"Fine. I'm fine." She knew she was smiling, knew the smile had a sad twist. And did not care. Here she could set aside her worries and her barriers and all the outside woes. Here was holy ground. "I was just wishing Poppa Joe could see us."

For some reason, no one showed surprise at her comment. Instead, they joined with her, sharing the same happy-sad, longing smile. Dawn said softly, "I've been thinking about him all night and I was afraid to say anything."

"I felt like he was sitting right here beside me," Duke agreed.

"I think Poppa Joe will be with us all for a while yet," Brian said. "A very long while."

Sadie served coffee and cake, and Hattie invited them to meet at her house the following week. Connie cooed over the baby with the others, listened as the Blackstones tried to express their appreciation to Nathan for his help, heard his shy acceptance. She felt deeply moved by the thought that dissolving his own angers had left him as exposed and uncertain as she felt herself.

As they slowly started getting ready to leave, Connie drew Dawn to one side and asked as casually as she could manage, "So how are things progressing about the wedding?"

"Oh, whew. I thought you were going to pester me again about the picnic this Sunday." Dawn let her hair fall into her face as she slid into her coat, but not before Connie caught sight of the nervous flicker in her eyes. "Things are going all right."

"Have you set a date?"

"Not yet." Dawn flipped her hair back, her nerves fully exposed. "Actually, things have been put on hold for a little while."

"They have?" Connie felt the attention of the entire room shift toward them. "Why?"

"Oh, hard to say."

"Go on, Dawn, honey," Duke said softly from his place by Nathan on the sofa. "It's time you asked."

"No, it's not." She tried to mask her fidgety nerves with quick gaiety. "You about ready to go?"

Connie watched the big man rise and walk over. "It's okay, sweetheart. Sooner or later you've got to do it," he said.

But Dawn's strength dissolved with a slumping of her shoulders and a lowering of her face. "No. I can't."

Connie felt her heart go out as she watched the tender way Duke wrapped his arm around Dawn's shoulders and held her close. She recalled the way Duke had spoken to the young boy at Poppa Joe's that day, and realized she had never accepted his gentleness as real. She observed the love in his face and the kind-hearted touch, and felt dirtied by her own blind jealousy.

Duke asked softly, "You want me to do it?"

Dawn responded with a little nod directed at the floor.

"All right." Duke turned his gaze toward Connie. "The

reason we haven't set a date is because Dawn doesn't want to get married unless you will be her maid of honor."

For a long moment Connie could not respond. She remained locked in place by a sudden thought. It struck her like a hammer-blow. Instead of being there and helping Dawn at this most important moment of her life, her defiant little girl had been reduced to slump-shouldered defeat by Connie's ill will. Connie felt pounded down to about three inches tall.

She swallowed her shame and said, "I would be honored."

Dawn lifted her face. "Really?"

The relief in Dawn's gaze left Connie feeling as if her heart were packed in ground glass. "Thank you so much for wanting me up there with you, honey."

Connie endured the hugs and the farewells, desperately eager to just get out and away. But when she stepped out on the porch, Nathan approached and asked, "Can I give you a lift?"

"I'm just down the street a ways."

"Mind if I walk with you?"

To her surprise, she found the honest answer to be, "I'd be grateful for the company."

The night closed in around them, still and crisp. The mountains cut shadow-lines from the starry sky, the ridges standing like timeless sentinels, there to protect and defend her little valley. Nathan spent a few moments walking in silence, his eyes on the night, before saying, "You seemed to be in quite a hurry to get out of there."

"I didn't feel like I deserved to be a part of their happiness just then," Connie confessed, and then found the rest of it bubbling out. How she had felt about Chad Campbell and the early days, how she had refused to marry him, how she had treated Dawn like her own daughter. How she had disliked Duke from the start. How she had never given him a chance. How she had never accepted how in truth she was still trying to hold on to what was never hers in the first place.

It was all quite a while in the telling, and when she finished Nathan kept on beside her, letting the night and the quiet road and the walk work its way in and calm her down. Finally he said, "We've overshot the mark a ways."

Connie looked around and realized her house was a half-mile behind them. "Why didn't you stop us?"

"You seemed to need the chance to air out some thoughts, and I liked listening to you talk."

She allowed Nathan to turn her back around, and began wondering if she had made a fool of herself by all she had just confessed to. But when he spoke again, it was to say, "I can't begin to tell you how different my life is here from before."

"Different good or different bad?"

"I'm not sure. I'm not even certain how to compare them." He formed a block with his hands over to his right. "Over there I had one of the top hospitals in the world. I worked inhuman hours, never had enough time, measured my life by the millisecond. It was a constant race, a never-ending battle. I did not know the patients except through the status of their illness. Their families either coped or were referred to counseling. Everything had its slot. And there was never enough time. Never."

He set another block in place in front of her. "Over here, now, we have my life in Hillsboro. I am beginning to know my patients as people. I have a sense of who they are, the lives they lead, their little dramas and worries and habits and foibles."

"We've got a lot of those," Connie offered.

"You do, you know. It's amazing. But at the same time, you have a nobility."

That drew her to a halt. "Come again?"

"It's true, Connie. I saw it most clearly in Poppa Joe, but it's there in so many of the people I see around here. I used to think what I was seeing was a little bit of him in each of them. A bit of his essence. But it's not his. That's what I was thinking about in the Bible study tonight." He stopped and looked down at her. "Am I making any sense at all?"

"I've just poured out my life's woes to you and you're asking *me* about making sense?" She reached over and grasped his hand, the movement not even conscious until she had done it. His grip was warm and soft and strong. "Go on. Tell me more."

His breath was a long stream of white in the starry light. "You people hold to what I've lost. What I've never had, if you want to know the truth. If somebody were to come to me and say, where would I find the true American spirit, I would send them here. To a town that clings to what has defined them and their forefathers for two hundred years. To a people who are stubborn and hardheaded and fiercely protective of their own. To a place where people *matter*, where time is there to be used, not a master that uses them." He hesitated a long moment, then added softly, "To a life that has a place in it for faith. And values. And caring for others so deeply that a loss or a joy known to one binds them all more closely together."

Connie felt the same sense of gathering stillness, a clenching of the night air until it was hard to draw enough breath to ask, "You're staying, aren't you? Here. In Hillsboro. With us."

He nodded slowly, his features showing a somber acceptance of a decision already taken in his heart. "Yes," he said, the night ringing with quiet force. "Yes. I think I've finally found myself a home."

She released his grasp so that she could run her hand up his arm and over his shoulder to the warm skin of his neck. "Nathan Reynolds, I do believe you may kiss me now."

Twenty-Eight

Connie carried her good feeling into sleep that night. It was there still with her first cup of coffee. It even managed to brighten the rainy day. Normally Connie hated days like these, when the mountains were short stubby nubs, cut off by clouds so heavy they couldn't lift themselves over the peaks. The roads ran like miniature rivers, and the valley acted like a funnel for every wet and frigid gust. But today the heart's smile shone like her own private sun.

Right until she pulled into Allen Motors and surveyed all the empty repair bays.

Earl, chief mechanic and wrecker driver, sauntered his way through the door leading to the dealership's offices. He was carrying a wrench in one hand and a cup of coffee in the other. He was talking back over his shoulder as

he stepped into the bays, which was why he did not see Connie at first. When he turned and spotted the Oldsmobile and recognized the driver, he released both hands simultaneously.

The wrench struck one toe, and the cup broke and splashed steaming coffee down the other pants leg. Which was how he came to be doing a rapid two-step as Connie got out of the car and started toward him. She was not smiling now. "Earl?"

"Ow, ow, jeepers creepers, that was hot. Morning, Miss Connie."

"Earl, where is Poppa Joe's truck?"

"These were my last pair of clean pants too. Miss Connie, we'll have it to you directly."

"I didn't ask you when it'd be ready, now did I?" She started forward, which caused Earl to two-step his way back toward the doorway. "I asked you *where it was*."

"Miss Connie, the truck . . . We've . . ." He bent over and swiped at his leg. "Doggone it, that was hot."

She knew anger was called for here. It was one of those times when the only way she was going to get results was to push, and push hard. But the anger simply wasn't there. She was no longer smiling, but she could feel that sense of lightness still with her. She sighed defeat at herself and said, "Tell me the truth, Earl."

"The truth. Why sure, Miss Connie." The lanky mountain man resigned himself to straightening up. He risked one glance in her direction, then his arms started waving and his eyes scattered glances like buckshot out of a bent barrel. "Miss Connie, we've done scoured the whole state for parts. Even got a piece from down Greensboro way, and that's the whole honest truth."

She crossed her hands. "You're not going to tell me where the truck is, are you?"

"I done worked on that truck harder than I've worked on anything in my entire life. Spent hours and hours under the hood, upside the rack, you name it, I been there. Twice."

"There's something going on here, I can smell it." But the smile was back, and not just at heart level. She had to frown just to keep the edges of her mouth from lifting up. "How much is all this going to cost?"

The eyeballs started moving so fast she could almost hear them click. "Now, Miss Connie, you know I don't have a thing to do with costing out work 'round here."

She was not going to get anything out of the man. "I'll be back here on Monday, Earl. That should give you time to find my truck."

His shoulders slumped with vast relief. "You do that, Miss Connie. Monday'll be just fine with me."

"You tell Fuller Allen that if he's thinking on padding my bill with extras I didn't agree to, he's got another think coming. Right upside his head."

But Earl was already backpedaling toward the doorway. "You have yourself a right good day, now, you hear?"

Connie had a thousand things waiting for her at the county building. A lot of the nonessentials had been left piled up since before the funeral, and she needed to get started on them. Even so, her car seemed to have a will of its own, and drove her from the garage straight over to the clinic. She sat there, watching the rain streak the windshield, wondering how it could seem so awkward and yet so right to be here. An uncommon lightness carried her up the clinic's front steps, her feet scarcely touching the ground. She pushed through the door, shook off the rain from her coat, hung it up, and turned to Hattie and the smirk she knew she would find there.

"Why, if it isn't Miss Connie Wilkes." Hattie was all eyes and teeth and delight over this change to her routine. "And just how might you be this fine day, Miss Wilkes?"

"Wet. Is Nathan in?"

If anything, the eyes grew bigger. "Why yes, I do believe *Nathan* might be around here somewhere." She folded her hands primly on her desk. "Shall I go ask if he can see you? I don't recall making an appointment for you, but I'm sure . . ."

Connie drew her face down close to the desk and murmured, "You're not half as cute as you think you are."

Hattie was not the least bit put off. "This moment ought to be frozen and framed, it's so priceless."

Connie started to retort, then decided it really wasn't necessary. Which seemed to surprise Hattie as much as it did her, for the woman moved back a fraction and lost the edge to her smirk as Connie seated herself in the chair across from her and leaned across the desk. "Nathan said something to me last night. I want you to know. He said he was thinking about staying here in Hillsboro."

What was left of Hattie's smirk vanished entirely. "Oh, thank the good Lord above."

"We don't know anything for certain, mind you. But that's what he told me." Connie glanced at the closed door. "I stopped by to see if what he said in the night still makes sense to him in the day."

Hattie rose as though ejected from her seat. "You come right on back with me to his office."

Connie followed her down the hall. She stood in the center of the office after Hattie had closed the door and gone for Nathan. Rain patted gently against the window. In the distance the swollen river rushed and rustled and called to her. The room smelled slightly musty, probably from the books lining the back wall. Connie walked over and inspected the dusty rows. She opened one at random, saw it was a medical text printed before the First World War.

The door opened behind her. "I really should get around to hauling those things off."

She snapped the book closed and sneezed as the dust rose in her face. "Excuse me."

"Bless you." Nathan took the book from her, put it back, and offered her a clean handkerchief. "Wipe off your hands."

"My momma used to say that was the mark of a real gentleman, if he was able to offer a lady a clean hankie."

He led her over to a chair and pulled up another beside her. "I would have liked to have met your parents, Connie."

"They would have positively swooned at the sight of you." She handed back the handkerchief, felt the smile unfolding in her heart, did not bother to mask it. "A tall, dark, and handsome young man who also happens to be a doctor." Then she stopped. "That sounded horrid and forward, didn't it?"

"You can't help but sound good. To me, anyway." He pulled his chair closer. "I got a call from Margaret Simmons this morning. She said for me to be sure and tell you hello. They're preparing a shipment of used equipment, it ought to be arriving next week. The hospital updates constantly, but what they're casting off is still light-years ahead of what I'm working with now."

"I'm so glad." There was such kindness in his gaze, such sorrow and compassion and happiness all mixed in there together that she could not help but reach over and touch his face. He raised his own hand and held hers where it was.

They sat there for a long moment, until Connie lowered her hand, taking his with her, and said, "I was wondering if your feelings about staying in Hillsboro had changed in the light of day." She glanced at the back window. "Such as it is."

Nathan shook his head. "I spent a lot of time last night thinking how glad I found myself here." He stopped. "I mean, that I found myself *coming* here."

"I know what you mean."

"There must be people who come to know themselves and God's peace in the city. But I didn't. I don't know if I ever would have. The battle was too much for me." He was silent a moment, then added, "I think it would take a very strong person to find peace in the city, and keep hold of it."

Connie leaned forward. "I think you're the strongest man I've ever met. In your own way. Poppa Joe felt the same."

He was genuinely surprised. "He did?"

"He told me. He said you were a man who hadn't discovered either your strength or your purpose, and he prayed that God would show you both."

While Nathan mulled that over, thunder rolled down the valley, causing the clinic to shiver. Connie watched his face, saw how her words warmed him. Gradually he drew himself up straighter. A further trace of the old sadness left his eyes. She felt herself shiver with the clinic, filled with joy over being able to bestow such a gift.

When she saw he was unable to carry on the conversation himself, she glanced again at the window and said, "I hope they have better weather for the picnic."

His gaze turned guarded. "You know about that?"

"I know the whole town is busy keeping a secret from me." She inspected his face. "You know what it is, don't try to tell me different. What is going on here?"

"Connie . . ." He sighed his resignation. "If you insist, I'll tell you. But I wish you'd just wait. Please."

Because it was Nathan who asked, and because her heart was already full of surprises, she answered him with a smile and a playful, "So how is it that you know about this secret surprise and I don't?"

"Because, well, it was my idea. Sort of. Part of it, anyway. The rest was Brian's."

Connie found it necessary to bite her lip before she could ask, "You thought up a surprise for me?"

Nathan started to respond, then saw the look she was giving him, and a new light came to his eyes. "Have you ever been kissed in a doctor's office before?"

When Connie told Nathan her farewells and walked back into the waiting room, she found the entire crowd watching her. Instantly she knew Hattie had told them. For once she did not mind the incredible speed with which news spread through this town.

When Connie stood by the door and said nothing, Hattie's hands gradually scrunched the paper she was holding into a tight wad. "Well?"

Connie took a breath. Despite the faint scents of illness and disinfectant and age, despite the closed-in odors of an overcrowded waiting room on a cold and rainy day, she felt as though the breath could go on forever. She smiled at

Hattie, at the room, at the folks, at the day. "Doctor Nathan Reynolds is going to stay in Hillsboro."

There was a sense of the whole room sharing in her breath, drawing in her smile. Hattie said weakly, "You're sure?"

"Sure as I can be of anything in this crazy world." She looked down at her friend and nodded her head. "I can't hardly believe it either."

Hattie permitted herself a shaky little laugh. "This is just plain wonderful."

"It's better than that," Connie said, feeling like they all must see the sun she felt rising in her heart. "It's a miracle."

Twenty-Nine

The day was a gift. And it just kept getting better.

The village church bells woke Nathan, ringing sweetly in the winter air. He went straight to his window and was astonished to find sunlight there to greet him. He reached for his watch, could not believe it actually read eight o'clock. Then he glanced back at the sunlight. And he laughed. The drenching rain was nothing but a memory, the future blazing with light and promise.

After church, Nathan rode up to Poppa Joe's with Dawn and Duke. People were honking and waving and shouting back and forth even before they left the parking lot. It seemed as though the entire town must have been either in front or behind them, there were so many cars and station wagons and pickups. They made their noisy way up the winding roads, waving at the occasional car coming down the other way, calling at them to turn around. Nonsense gaiety, no reason for it other than the fact that it was a beautiful day for a winter gathering.

Duke and the other young men had been busy all week, and it showed. The branches were cut back from the uphill track, and the worst of the gullies had been filled in with fresh gravel. Even so, he was hanging on and whooping with the others as they powered up the steepest bit and crested the final rise.

A large swatch of meadow had been mowed and lined with rope, designating the makeshift parking area. They left the truck, carrying baskets and blankets and bags. Kids and dogs went streaming by, filling the hillside meadow with their racket.

Trestle tables had been carted up and settled in long lines over beside Poppa Joe's old cabin. A pair of thick-chested mountain men with beards and long hair tended a huge barbecue pit. They would have looked dangerous save for the aprons and the laughter and the light in their eyes. Mothers stayed busy keeping the kids off Poppa Joe's porch and away from the huge tarpaulin-covered bundle there in front of the cabin. Nathan found himself shaking hands with people he had never seen before, talking with them as easily as he would his oldest friends. It was just that kind of day.

"Here she comes!"

The call brought them all around. The chatter died as though it had been cut off with a knife. The meadow was suddenly so quiet they could hear the doors slam in the distance and then Connie's voice cry out, "Let go of that basket, Hattie! It's bad enough we had to get up here last. I'm not an invalid. Now give me something to carry!"

It was enough to set the entire gathering to howling with laughter. Nathan found himself slapping a total stranger's back, wiping his eyes, agreeing with one of Will Green's musicians that it was definitely Connie over there. Yessir. The one and only.

They grew quiet again, though, when Connie got close enough for them to see her face. They watched her take in the huge bulk wrapped in canvas there before the porch, then glance at all the faces smiling her way. Her shoulders tucked in a little, as though she were too uncertain under all that scrutiny to be her normal assertive self.

"Nathan? Where's the doc?" Fuller Allen stepped through the crowd, spotted Nathan by one of the tables, and waved at him. "Get on over here, Doc. This here's your doing."

"No, it's not." But he started walking anyway. "Earl's the one who did it."

"Earl supplied the sweat. You gave us the idea." When he was up close, Fuller swept Nathan up in one arm and said, "Connie, honey, we've got something for you."

She tried for a little of the old bluster, but her nerves showed with the trembling in her voice. "Who's we?"

"Near 'bout everybody you see here. We all chipped in a little." Fuller was beaming so hard his red-cheeked face looked ready to split like an overripe fruit. "It's our way of saying thank you, honey."

She crossed her arms, squinted at the canvas, then said, "I haven't done a thing worth getting thanked for."

"Sure you have. You've seen us through thick and thin." The hand squeezed Nathan's shoulders. "Why, you even brought us Doc here."

Nathan found himself glancing around the circle of faces, those in jackets and those in coveralls, those with strength and youth, those with beards and weather-beaten features, those who wore poverty like a second skin. He saw some gap-toothed smiles, and some deeply creased features. He saw how some of the kids stood and watched while others ran in the distance shrieking with the joy of the day. Not patients to be catalogued and treated. People. His people. The people of his home.

Fuller Allen drew him back with, "Go on, Nathan, open her up."

Nathan started to object, then decided, "Earl, come on over here and give me a hand."

The lanky mechanic was blushing to the roots of his hair as he walked forward and took hold of one corner of the tarpaulin. Together they started drawing it off, walking slowly backward so they could watch as the truck came into view and see Connie's expression at the same time.

Connie's mouth opened and stayed that way. Her eyes widened, and grew wider still. Nathan looked from her to the truck, then to the people watching and grinning, and back to Connie.

Then he did what felt natural. He clapped Earl on the shoulder and he said loud enough for all to hear, "You've done yourself proud. That is one beautiful truck."

Earl beamed and replied, "Ain't she, though?"

Connie took a little step toward the truck. Somebody called, "Go on, honey, she won't bite."

Hesitantly she reached forward and touched the polished sky-blue surface. The truck positively gleamed. The newly galvanized surfaces shone like solid silver.

Connie opened the door. It swung on new hinges. In fact, the entire truck was almost completely new, right down to the wheels and rims. Nathan watched as Connie leaned into the truck, felt the old steering wheel, and took a long shaky breath. When she turned back around, her eyes were brimming over and her throat was so tight she was barely able to say, "It still smells like him."

That was enough to bring them all around. They laughed and crowded up and congratulated Earl and clapped Nathan's back and chattered and exclaimed. Nathan could not recall ever having seen so many smiles in one place before.

The lunch was long and lazy and noisy. Nathan sat at a table across from Connie, but they scarcely spoke to one another. Having so many people around left them both a little bashful. Every once in a while she would look over at him, though, and give him a glance that melted his heart.

Finally Brian Blackstone rose to his feet and raised his hands for silence. Nathan found his gaze snagged by Sadie, who was seated there beside him, the baby nestled in her arms. As the crowd quieted for Brian, the baby gave a chortling laugh. Since the eating problem had been resolved, Nathan had never known a happier baby. *His people.*

"I'd like to thank everybody for making this the finest picnic I think I've ever been on," Brian said. When the applause and chatter died down again, he went on, "But there's one more thing to do before this day is over."

"That's right," a woman called out. "Clean up this mess!"

"Okay, okay," Brian said, quieting them. "Two things, then." He turned his smile toward Nathan. "Our Nathan has asked if we would baptize him up here in Poppa Joe's lake."

Someone farther down the table said something to Nathan, and he looked down and smiled his reply. But he really did not hear them. His mind was held by two words the pastor had said. *Our Nathan.* It was the most remarkable title he had ever been given. A prize to carry with him all his life long. *Our* Nathan.

Then he looked back at Connie and saw the tears streaming down her face. It was hard, but he knew he had to do it then, walk around in front of all of those people and raise her up and take her in his arms. She buried her face in his shoulder, shaking her head back and forth as she wiped her eyes and her cheeks. Nathan felt his face go flush at the sound of all those people laughing and clapping at them. But he held on just the same.

When he started to release her, she took a grip on his hand that kept him close, and she turned and sniffled and called out, "Dawn, Duke, come over here a minute."

As the pair of them approached, Nathan wondered at the wary look they gave Connie. But she just sniffed again and wiped her face another time, and said loud enough for all nearby to hear, "I was meaning to do it all up legal and proper first. But there won't be a better time than this."

She reached over and took hold of Duke's hand with her free one. The act caused both Dawn and Connie's chins to quiver. She squeezed the hand firmly and she said in a loud voice, "I'm giving you a piece of Poppa Joe's meadow as your wedding present. I want you to build yourselves a home up here."

The noise spread out in a grand wave of surprise, but the center remained utterly still. The couple's faces there before Nathan were shocked to silence. Connie gave Duke's hand a little shake and said, "He would have wanted this. I know it for sure and for certain."

Then before they could recover enough to speak, she turned back to Nathan, and said, "All right. It's your time now." And she hugged him again. "You are a good man, Nathan Reynolds. A good man."

Nathan carried that with him as Brian motioned him over and asked, "We usually like to have a little hymn to start us on our way. Do you have a favorite?"

"As long as I don't have to sing," Nathan replied, and waited until the chuckles stilled to add, "I'd love to hear Will give us, 'I Will Arise and Go to Jesus.'"

As they all rose and started off behind Brian, Will's bow scratched across the strings, and once more the voices rose and chimed out the timeless words. The sun was so bright that the day was not permitted to hold even a trace of winter chill. The meadow was a golden sea, the mountains alive and echoing with their own response to the hymn.

Nathan walked there between Brian and Connie, down the path that led into the forest, and the hymn and the people followed along behind. As he walked through the sweet-scented woods, he felt as though Poppa Joe had suddenly sauntered over to walk with him. And Nathan knew he would never forget this. Not even if he lived a thousand years.

They came out into the clearing, and the people stretched all the way around the lake's stony rim. Nathan stepped into the lake there beside Brian, not minding in the least how cold the water felt. It seemed as though the sun itself had come down to reside there among the people. For this moment, this instant of timeless perfection, the light of heaven became a reality so strong it joined to his heart, and united all the pieces of life and dreams into a new and certain whole. For this moment, though his mind would ask new questions every day remaining to him on this earth, all the mysteries of life were calmed, and all the wounds healed.

Then Brian placed his hands on Nathan's head, and spoke a prayer that Nathan both heard and could not hear. He allowed the pastor to lower him down, down, down and into the cold clear lake.

He found it amazing, how the light came into the water with him.

OTHER GREAT BOOKS FROM T. DAVIS BUNN

The Warning

As Buddy Korda stared at the page in front of him, the words rose up with new and terrifying meaning. The nightmares he'd been having started to make sense. And then, unmistakably, a message. The futures of people he didn't even know — the future of the nation — were at stake, if he didn't answer God's call. But what would happen if no one believed him?

0-7852-7516-9 • Trade Paperback • 288 pages

Tidings of Comfort and Joy

This endearing story starts with an old photograph — one of Marissa's grandmother taken during World War II, younger and more beautiful than she had ever seen. But the officer who was embracing her with such passion — he didn't look like her grandfather. As the questions begin, an extraordinary story unfolds. A story of love and loss and caring, of separation and reunion, this novella is destined to become a holiday classic as well as a wonderful family story.

0-7852-7203-8 • Hardcover • 240 pages

To the Ends of the Earth

A compelling historical tale of political, religious, and personal conflict during the rise of Christianity. The favorite son of a Carthaginian merchant journeys to Constantinople to find riches and power. But when he finds ruthless government ruling in the name of Christendom, his faith and his life are in danger.

0-7852-7214-3 • Trade Paperback • 408 pages